Praise for *Soul Food*

Quirky characters, surprising plots and complex history come together in this inspiring collection of stories. *Soul Food* is written with heart, thought and wit that will make you think, laugh and learn; a delightful read.

Nancy Slonim Aronie, author of *Writing from the Heart* and *Memoir as Medicine*

Soul Food is a delightful collection of stories, chock full of humor, each one infused with a salient essence of truth. Each offering feeds the soul and nourishes the spirit. Pair with tea, espresso or a fine wine.

Phyllis A. Blackstone, educator, storyteller and author of *My Storied Life*

Reading *Soul Food* by Beth Gibbs was like sharing a delicious meal with old friends. Each story is a delectable dish, served up by appealing, clever characters—people I felt I knew or wished I knew. A variety of timely topics are part of the friendly dinner conversation. Beth's clear, concise writing style makes each story a pleasure to read. While each story stands on its own, I particularly enjoyed the way threads and characters of one story found their way into other stories, much like the flavors and spices of a good meal are picked up throughout several dishes. I finished the collection feeling content and satisfied, as though I'd eaten an enjoyable meal.

Carla Dean, President, Journey Writers, Inc.

Soul Food

Other Books by the Author

Ogi Bogi the Elephant Yogi

Enlighten Up!

Soul Food

Life-Affirming Stories
Served with Side Dishes
and Just Desserts

by

Beth Gibbs

Sherman, Connecticut

Soul Food:
Life-Affirming Stories Served with Side Dishes and Just Desserts

Books published by Emerald Lake Books may be ordered through your favorite booksellers or by visiting emeraldlakebooks.com.

Library of Congress Cataloging-in-Publication Data

Names: Gibbs, Beth, author.

Title: Soul food : life-affirming stories served with side dishes and just desserts / by Beth Gibbs.

Description: Sherman, Connecticut : Emerald Lake Books, [2022] |

Identifiers: LCCN 2022037034 (print) | LCCN 2022037035 (ebook) | ISBN 9781945847660 (trade paperback) | ISBN 9781945847677 (epub)

Subjects: LCSH: Self-consciousness (Awareness)--United States. | Affirmations--United States. | African Americans--Social conditions.

Classification: LCC BF311 .G475 2022 (print) | LCC BF311 (ebook) | DDC 153.4--dc23/eng/20220912

LC record available at https://lccn.loc.gov/2022037034

LC ebook record available at https://lccn.loc.gov/2022037035

This book is dedicated to three women whose lives and wisdom have shaped my own.

Margaret Jackson Gibbs, my mother (1908–2010).
Mom was strong-willed, vital and resolute.
She taught me the value of independence
and self-determination.

Lucille Ellen Garnett, my great-aunt (1892–1962),
who was independent, self-sufficient
and the first Black woman to own and drive a car
in our small New England town.

Ella I. Garnett, my second cousin (1924–2016).
Ella was a larger-than-life personality whose humor, life
and relationship wisdom I still follow and pass on to others.

Contents

Note to My Readers

Dear Reader,

Soul Food is a collection of loosely connected, life-affirming stories celebrating the tenacity of the human spirit in seeking and finding clarity, contentment and resilience in a complicated world. The stories span chronological, emotional and thematic arcs dotted with humor and moments of self-reflection. Some were inspired by real historical incidents that have been fictionalized. The rest are pure fiction.

You can read the stories in any order, as each stands on its own, or follow them from first to last to discover connections between the characters, their struggles and their relationships with each other. For example:

- In "A Recipe for Freedom," Rebecca publishes a cookbook entitled *The Art of Nutmeg Cookery*. In it is a recipe for gingerbread that reappears in "A Grave Situation" and "A Party for Allen."
- In "A Grave Situation," we meet Lucille Jenkins who confronts the undertaker handling her husband's funeral arrangements. In "Waiting for Grace," she counsels her brother. Then we meet her again as the wise cousin in "How Sadie Smoked 'Em" and as Allen's mother in "A Party for Allen."

- In "The Lady in Red," Larry and Marilyn Winston discover the body of a woman in a glass coffin on their estate. Shared history related to the mystery then resurfaces in "Mama Rose's Kitchen" during a political struggle on the other side of town.
- In "The Enlightenment of Franklin Rutledge," the title character, a divorced, middle-aged, self-absorbed psychiatrist, starts the journey to his own healing. Along the way, he helps Martha Rae Edmonds in "The Well-Wrapped Life" and Delores in "1-800-555-MARY."
- In "Warrior Women of The Third Sunday," we meet Claudette from "A Stitch in Time"; Marceline, Franklin Rutledge's ex-wife from "The Enlightenment of Franklin Rutledge"; and several other women from previous stories as they gather for their monthly book club meeting.

THESE DIVERSE and sometimes quirky characters must navigate the ups and downs of their lives by meeting a challenge, making a change, consciously choosing not to change, or finding acceptance and peace if change is not possible.

The discussion questions at the end of the book are designed to help you, your friends or your book club think about and discuss the connections and relationships between the characters, as well as their journeys to self-awareness on their quest to find clarity, contentment and resilience. This section also contains a glossary of some cultural terms that may be unfamiliar to you.

Like a good Sunday brunch, which includes complimentary foods from appetizers to desserts, the stories are colorful, homey, easily digested and filling for mind, body and spirit.

Enjoy *Soul Food*—and come back for seconds!

A Recipe for Freedom

This story is about two independent women, one Black and one White, caught in the economic, social and cultural prejudices of nineteenth-century America. Despite their differences, the two women encourage each other to gain freedom, independence and self-determination. The recipe in the story is typical of wedding cakes from the 1800s.

The knock at the door sounded firm and determined. Rebecca took a deep breath, let it out with a sigh, and tucked a few strands of corkscrew curls into the bun at the back of her head. Thirty years of silence were about to end.

"Just a minute!" Rebecca cried. She needed that minute to still her beating heart, shaking hands, and racing thoughts.

I'm a free woman. I own my home and my catering business. It's doin' well despite the new hotels and restaurants springin' up all over. The rich folks ain't gonna let a thirty-year-old mystery stand in the way of good food and drink, even if it does involve one of their own gone missin' back in 1859. If trouble comes, I'll pack up, go to Canada, and start over with my sister's help.

She took the flour tin from the cabinet, placed it next to the other ingredients on the kitchen table, straightened her shoulders, arranged her full lips into a welcoming smile, and opened the door.

Rebecca took in Charles Bernard's bushy eyebrows, handlebar mustache, and short-trimmed beard sprinkled with gray. His demeanor was straightforward and nonthreatening, and the tension in her shoulders and around her lips eased.

Charles, a reporter from the *Baltimore Sun,* stepped into the kitchen and tipped his hat. "Miss Rebecca, I cannot thank you enough for your message and for finally agreeing to meet with me after all these years. I am honored."

Rebecca offered Charles a cup of tea and a seat at the table. He accepted the beverage, thanked her, and sat down. "May I ask what happened to change your mind?"

She handed him the letter.

His eyes skimmed it quickly, locked onto the signature, and shot back up to meet hers.

"So she's alive. I always thought so. Finally, we can learn how." He smiled. "Shall we get started?"

"Yes," said Rebecca. "We can talk whilst I make this weddin' cake for Mr. Edwards's daughter. She's gettin' married on Saturday."

Rebecca grated nutmeg, cinnamon, cloves and mace into a fragrant pile.

"That's a fine looking grater you're using," said Charles. "Silver, isn't it?"

Rebecca glanced up from the growing heap of spices and smiled. "Yes, and it's special to me. It's a gift from Mr. and Mrs. Edwards. They were real grateful, 'cause after I started cookin' at Tavern House, business went way up. It got to be the place to go for travelers and folks seekin' good company, good food and the latest gossip. Hear the scratchy sound from the gratin'? It's soothin', and back then when it happened, I needed soothin'. What me and Miss Margaret did was risky.

If anythin' went wrong, I'd a ended up in big trouble, with no future, no money and no help. She woulda been ruint!"

Rebecca deftly scooped the spices into an earthenware bowl and sifted a bit of flour into the mixture.

She watched Charles take a few sheets of paper from his leather satchel, as well as his steel-pointed pen and an inkwell.

With his right hand poised to write, he asked, "Can we begin with your story?" After Rebecca nodded her assent, Charles posed his first question. "How did you happen to come to Baltimore?"

"Well, me, my parents and my older sister, Sarah, were in bondage on a rice plantation in South Carolina. Then Daddy got sold away to a cotton plantation in Georgia. A few months later, Mama got sold off. We never found out where. Then Sarah got sold to a tobacco plantation in Virginia. A year later, when I was ten, I got sold to Mr. and Mrs. Pickett in Maryland. They had a grand house in Baltimore. They wanted me as a companion for their daughter, who was seven. So me and Miss Margaret grew up like sisters, 'ceptin' for the fact I was her servant at the same time as I was her companion."

As she spoke, Rebecca creamed butter and sugar together in a separate bowl.

"Sounds like a difficult time for you," said Charles.

Rebecca sighed and shook her head. "Didn't matter if it was or wasn't. It was my life. I couldn't change it. I couldn't leave. I was missin' my parents and my sister somethin' awful. It was what it was, but even so, I had it better than many. I lived as best I could at the time. I mighta been in bondage, bein' legally owned by Miss Margaret's daddy, but my insides have always been my own."

Picking up a spoon, she mixed raisins, currants, citron and chopped almonds together in another bowl.

"Anyway, what you're lookin' to write about started when Miss Margaret was 'bout sixteen. Her parents been actin' mysterious for weeks, so when they went into the library one evenin', curiosity bested us and we snuck up to the door so we could hear what they'd been about. Sounded serious—Mr. Pickett bein' quiet-like and Mrs. Pickett yellin'. When footsteps started toward the door, we hightailed it to the kitchen. Mrs. Pickett found us there, asked Miss Margaret to come with her, and told me to stay in the kitchen. I could tell Miss Margaret was gettin' upset—and turns out with good reason.

"See, Mr. Pickett was in the middle of talkin' marriage for Miss Margaret to an associate in his shipbuildin' business. He was wantin' to keep the business in the family, and since he didn't have a son, he wanted to pick his son-in-law. Miss Margaret and her momma fought him somethin' terrible. Neither one a them liked Mr. Tobias. He'd been to dinner a few times. Miss Margaret told me he had shifty eyes and sweaty hands, but in the end, she gave in and got married to Mr. Tobias."

Rebecca slowly dredged the fruits and nuts with some more flour, her shoulders hunched with the weight of the memory.

"Why did she agree?"

"She didn't agree. She kinda had no choice. She didn't wanna be an old maid. She had a social standin' to uphold for the family, and it woulda been unheard of for her to work. To me, it seemed, despite her family's wealth and social standin', she didn't have much more freedom than me. Sure, she could dress up and visit friends, spend lazy afternoons drinking tea and workin' on her embroidery. Maybe nobody owned her like they owned me. But it didn't make a whole lotta difference in the end."

Charles looked up from his notes. "That must have been a difficult time for her."

Swallowing hard, Rebecca stirred together the spices, fruits and nuts with the rest of the flour.

"It was hard for both of us. I was scared and upset, too, all the to-do about the weddin' and no one sayin' anythin' about what would happen to me, and me not havin' the right to ask or say anythin'. Finally, Miss Margaret told me I was gonna be part of her new household. I guess you could say I was nothin' more than a livin', breathin' weddin' gift. I wasn't happy about it and it wasn't all smiles and roses in the new household, but Miss Margaret and I got on well enough despite the difficulty."

"What kind of difficulty?" asked Charles as he drained the last of his tea.

"I was servin' three masters. One, Mr. Tobias. And Mr. Tobias, God rest his soul, was not a nice man. I had to come up with all kinda ways to avoid him 'cause he wanted more from me than cookin' and cleanin', if you know what I mean."

Charles nodded. He knew.

"Two, Miss Margaret. I helped with her dressin', her hair, and keepin' the house runnin' smooth, but the old ease between us wasn't there anymore. And then there was Mr. and Mrs. Edwards. See, Mr. Tobias rented me out to the Tavern House to cook for the lunch crowd, holidays and special events. He took all my earnin's. Said it was to pay him for my room, board and keep."

Rebecca vigorously beat eggs and molasses into the butter and sugar, scowling as she recalled the story.

"Anyway, despite the courtin' and sweet-talkin' to get Miss Margaret to marry him, he turned mean right after the weddin'. Like night and day he was! Never knew what could set him off. He was mean to both of us, but he beat her like I'm beatin' these eggs into this batter. She was so unhappy. After a while, she was desperate to leave, but she couldn't. If she'd a left on her own, it woulda ruined her reputation and damaged her family's social and economic standin'. There's no secrets among the upper crust in Baltimore. Folks woulda had a fine time whisperin' and gossipin'."

Shaking her head, Rebecca added brandy, wine and buttermilk to the butter, sugar, eggs and molasses.

"There was only one person she could ask for help. Me. See, I'd been tryin' to figure out how to get outta Mr. Tobias's house and be on my own. Turns out cookin' at Tavern House showed me the way, and Miss Margaret agreed to help me if I'd help her.

"She worked real hard to convince Mr. Tobias to make a deal with Mr. Edwards so I could buy my freedom and work at the tavern full time. At first, he resisted 'cause the idea came from Miss Margaret. But in the end, he agreed 'cause it would save him money. See, the law at the time said slave owners had to take care of their slaves when they got sick or old, so's they wouldn't be a burden on the public. But once a slave was freed, that went away. So Mr. Tobias agreed. I left his house to live and work at the Tavern House. This time, most of my earnin's went to pay back Mr. Edwards for buyin' my freedom, but I saved some too!"

Eyes brightening, Rebecca slowly folded the fruits, nuts, spices and flour mixture into the liquid ingredients.

"Miss Margaret was mostly always kind and helpful to me whilst I was in bondage in her house and in her parents' house, and now she needed some kindness and help from me. Thinkin' back on it, there I was, enjoyin' my freedom whilst she had limits, troubles and a different sorta not-being-free situation. She needed help, and I was her only lifeline. Funny, isn't it?"

Charles smiled his acknowledgment. "What happened then?"

Rebecca smiled as she scraped the batter into three papered baking hoops.

"A lot, Mr. Bernard. A lot. We put our heads together for weeks before we come up with a plan. We set our sights on makin' a cookbook. And the first problem was money—we needed some. Everythin' Miss Margaret had was Mr. Tobias's once they got married. She couldn't ask him or her family without rousin' suspicion. Everythin' I had was to care for myself and pay back Mr. Edwards, but it was clear to me I was gonna have to trust in God and use some of my savin's to help Miss Margaret get away, since she'd helped me get free."

Rebecca set the hoops in the brick oven, wiped her hands on her apron, and sat down at the table.

"Now, I couldn't read nor write back then, and Miss Margaret couldn't cook a lick, but between the two of us, we got it done. And we did all of it while Mr. Tobias was at work, since gettin' caught woulda been scary awful for both of us.

"I'd tell Miss Margaret the recipes, and she'd write 'em down. No one could know she had anythin' to do with it, so she coached me good. I took the papers to the printin' place. They typeset the pages and pretty soon we had us a book! We called it *The Art of Nutmeg Cookery* and put an engravin' of my grater on the cover. Inside was every recipe usin' nutmeg known to man, and some new ones I worked up in Mr. Edwards's kitchen. Thank heaven our cookbook flew outta the hands of the booksellers like hot johnnycakes!"

"Why nutmeg recipes?" asked Charles with a puzzled look.

"Back then, folk used nutmeg in everythin', from baked apples and cakes to pies, lamb chops and mulled wine. Every kitchen had a nutmeg tin and grater in the cupboard. It seemed like a good way to go, and it was! I made enough to pay myself back and give some money to Miss Margaret. Then, one night, while Mr. Tobias was out, I helped her pack her bags and got her to the Baltimore station and put her on the Underground Railroad."

"Why the Underground Railroad? I thought the railroad was for runaway slaves. Couldn't she take the train, or a boat from Chesapeake Bay Harbor?"

"Well, Mr. Bernard, with her family bein' so well-known, she woulda been spotted for sure. Mr. Tobias woulda tracked her down, brought her back, and beat her somethin' awful. Her father wasn't gonna do anythin' because he cared more about his business than he did 'bout his daughter. Disguisin' her mighta worked, but a young woman travelin' alone raises suspicion. We thought about me goin' with her as a companion, but back then any Black person leavin' Baltimore had to be checked, double-checked and signed for by a White person. We couldn't chance it. Too dangerous. The safest bet was the Underground Railroad. It woulda helped me to freedom if I wasn't already free, so I figured it would be good for freeing her too!"

"How did you arrange it? Did you have help?"

"Oh, yes. The Maryland Anti-Slavery Society was only too happy to help us once I told them how Miss Margaret had helped me. They had to get her to Philadelphia first. The guides said the best way was goin' along the Indian trails by foot and horseback. It was gonna be a long, hard trip. They told us it would take 'bout three or four days and said it was the best way to stay outta sight. Miss Margaret was awful scared but plenty determined.

"I knew she could rest up in Philadelphia before gettin' passed from station to station all the way up the East Coast to Canada. Sarah, my sister, had escaped from Virginia and was livin' in Montreal with her husband and their kids, so I gave Miss Margaret their address and told her to go find Sarah as soon as she got to Montreal."

"And then," said Charles, "you covered your tracks by dropping a pair of her shoes, a petticoat and a dress by the Patapsco River to fake suicide by drowning."

"Yessir. Her parents were shocked and grieved. Mr. Tobias didn't believe it. A great hue and cry come up, and the police got involved. They searched the area for days and dragged the river, but of course, never found a body. They questioned me a lotta times, but hidin' and lyin' comes natural when you've been in bondage since you could walk upright. My lips have been sealed shut for thirty years.

"Miss Margaret wanted to wait till both her parents were dead before settin' the record straight. So when I got her letter, I remembered it was you covered the story when it happened. I figured you'd want the truth be told, so the case got closed once and for all."

Charles put his pen down and sat back in his chair. A satisfied smile spread across his face, lighting up his blue eyes. "I knew it! My reporter's instincts told me there was more to the story. That's why I never gave up trying to talk to you, Miss Rebecca. I'm glad to know she's alive and well and living in Canada."

Rebecca folded her hands in her lap. With a solemn look, she raised her eyes to his and replied, "Yessir, she made a new life for herself there, and I made mine here. I guess you could say me and Miss Margaret made up our own recipe for freedom."

A Grave Situation

The source for this story is a joke. Seriously! When I heard it, I cracked up laughing and never forgot it. A year later, it resurfaced in this story, along with a liberal dose of soulful graveyard humor.

Lucille Jenkins was a shrewd and fiercely independent woman. The two thick braids curling around her ears like ram's horns gave her bulldog face an air of ferocity. She grew up big, dirt poor and determined to "get somewheres in this life." And she succeeded.

Her fierce determination got her a job as a demonstration cook for the local gas company, helped her raise two sons, and gained her status as the first woman in the county, Black or White, to own and drive a car. By all accounts, Lucille Jenkins was a woman of substance, much of it from having loved and outlived three husbands with good insurance policies: Frank Washington, Norman Paddyfoot and most recently Samuel Lenworth Jenkins.

It was "the bitters" that killed Sam. He was deeply, quietly angry and righteously bitter at a world refusing to look beneath his leathery black surface and respect his manhood. The bitterness festered in his gut for fifty-two years and, finding no way out, finally shot up his spine, smacked him in the head, exploded his brain, and contorted his face into a death mask that was terrible to see. The doctor called it a cerebrovascular accident. The nurse told Lucille it was a stroke. But Lucille knew it was the bitters.

She saw the signs and begged Sam to look past things he couldn't control. Happiness is in the little things of the here and now, she said. Sam listened because he loved her, but he could not do what she asked, and so he died.

Sam's inability to follow her advice tried Lucille's patience when he was alive, but his burial was trying her patience now.

He'd been dead and buried for two months, and she still hadn't paid the undertaker for the funeral. Indeed, she had no intention of paying him. She was furious about the way Homer Wilson had laid Sam out for the wake.

Sam's burial had also tried Homer's patience. Grieving women usually depended upon him to make appropriate arrangements and handle the gruesome details of death. Homer did his level best to relieve them of difficulties, unpleasantness and as much of their insurance money as possible.

Lucille Jenkins, however, was cut from a different cloth. He smelled trouble the moment Sam's body arrived at his funeral parlor. He'd done the best he could, trying to spare her from the embarrassment of having folks see Sam's face all rigid and twisted, but when he handed her the bill after the burial, she simply tucked it into her handbag instead of writing a check.

As she snapped the clasp shut, he glimpsed a hint of steel in her eyes. A resolute tightness in her unsmiling lips told him his sense of smell hadn't been wrong.

Homer and Lucille lived in a small, close-knit, rural southern community where privacy was as rare as hen's teeth. So it wasn't long before the dispute between them went public. Everyone watched with interest as Lucille and Homer squared off and began recruiting.

One afternoon, Lucille invited Pearl Smoot over to "set a spell."

"I told him to make sure my Sam looked natural. Natural! Well, Sam didn't look natural... Not natural at all."

Lucille cut Pearl a thick slice of her special nutmeg-glazed gingerbread. The recipe was from *The Art of Nutmeg Cookery*, a treasured cookbook passed down from her great-grandaunt Rebecca that now was in Lucille's possession, along with the family Bible. Lucille handed Pearl the plate and went on.

"Made him up to look like some pious jackleg preacher. And you know, sure as the world turns, Sam Jenkins was a whole lotta things, but he was not pious. No, sir! He done his share of drinkin', cussin' and card playin', but he was a natural man. A natural man, Pearl!"

Lucille poured Pearl a tall glass of fresh buttermilk.

"You saw how much powder and paint Homer put on him. Had his mouth pulled up in some apple-cheeked, half-moon smile the likes of which never crossed his lips in life. An' here come Homer tellin' me the nature of Sam's demise left him no choice. Pish tosh, my Aunt Minnie! To make matters worse, it were too late to do anythin' 'bout it 'cause folk was comin' in to pay their respects. I had to swallow the fit I had ready for Homer and do the right thing. But pay him? For ruinin' the way I last saw my Sam? I think not!" Her braids quivered with indignation, and her jowls wobbled with fury.

Pearl, whose gentle demeanor belied her reputation as a vicious gossip, nibbled daintily at a piece of gingerbread. She wiped a corner of her mouth with her napkin, spread it neatly on her lap, and purred, "Now, Lucille, you know Homer likes to put a positive face on death. And Sam, of all people, needed a smile on his face to meet his maker. I don't think you should be so hard on Homer, dear. He was just doing his job."

"Maybe so, Pearl, maybe so. But Sam was my husband before he was Homer's job, so I think he could've talked to me before taking my personal matters into his funeralizin' hands."

Lucille bid Pearl farewell, knowing her story would be all over town before morning. A hearty laugh passed her lips as she took the leavings of Pearl's visit to the kitchen, where Sam's dog, Boy-Boy, lay with his head drooped on his front paws, deep in doggy depression. *Poor li'l fella,* thought Lucille, scratching the spaces behind his floppy ears. *He misses Sam.* She fed him the last of the gingerbread.

Meanwhile, Homer held court at the barbershop. His throne was a ripped leather chair in the middle of Smitty's converted garage. His audience was the weekly throng gathered to "get right" for Saturday night at Big Jack's Honky Tonk or for Sunday morning services at Mount Moriah Baptist Church, depending upon each man's inclination, interest and intention. He regaled them with stories of how he planned to get his money and teach Lucille a lesson to boot. Smitty applied shaving cream to Homer's moving jowls while he spoke.

"Sam was too easy with her, you know." One manicured hand waved over the gathering like a papal blessing. "Let her have her way in too many of their affairs. Settin' a bad example for the rest of us."

Some men nodded, others smiled, and the rest remained unmoved, waiting to side with the winner so they could say, "I knew it all along." The diamond ring on Homer's pinky finger caught the light from the garage's 100-watt bulb and sparkled. His head bobbed up and down.

"Humph! It ain't right. I'll take her to court if I have to! Messin' wit' me. She need a good comeuppance."

Lucille knew Homer would not take her to court. It might've been the 1950s rather than the 1850s, but Black folk in Spotsylvania, Virginia, took care of minor disputes among themselves. Lucille intended to outwait and outwit Homer.

Homer, meanwhile, intended to get his money by any means necessary and save face in the bargain.

Despite his bravado in front of his cronies at the barbershop, he did not want to face Lucille himself. His reluctance had nothing to do with fear; it was more like discomfort. He knew he was evenly matched, and he didn't relish being evenly matched with a woman. It unsettled him. Homer was uncomfortable about pulling out the stops and handling the situation like he would if he were facing a man. After all, men understood how the game should be played, and they followed the rules. You could trust them. But he didn't trust Lucille to understand, much less follow, the rules of a confrontation. He was dealing with an unknown.

When the bill had gone unpaid for several months, he turned to his younger brother, Ernest.

"Aw, naw!" said Ernest when Homer approached him.

"Now, Ernest, you know we can't have that bill outstandin'. It gives folk ideas. If she gets away with it, others might try, and then someone's pay might be affected." He leaned into Ernest's personal space. "Know what I mean?"

Ernest knew. Reluctant feet carried his resistant body to Lucille's house to ask her for the money. But his resistance soon melted, faster than a pig gobbling slop because each time he showed up, Lucille smiled sweetly and invited him in for fried chicken and biscuits or a piece of fresh baked apple pie. She'd tell him the money would be along in a few days.

"I'll settle with your brother as soon as I get over the worst of my grievin' and can put my mind to business matters. You understand, Ernest?"

"Oh, yes'm," said Ernest as his mouth opened to receive a huge forkful of apple pie. "Yes'm, I surely do. I surely do, indeed." Ernest's stomach was on the receiving end of some mighty fine cooking, and he was only too happy to play messenger between Lucille and his brother.

When Ernest, after several trips to Lucille's, had brought back nothing but excuses, a satisfied smile, and a few extra pounds around his middle, Homer finally put his squeamishness aside and went to see her himself. He arrived at her front gate one Sunday with his hat in hand, a thin veneer of respect in his voice, and cunning in his eyes.

From her parlor window, Lucille watched him open the front gate and slither in. Like a bolt of greased lightning, she shot into position on the top step of her front porch, so he'd have to look up at her from the walk. Homer conceded the point with a nod of his head, fixed his eyes on hers, and began the skirmish.

"Afternoon, Miz Jenkins. How're you?"

"Why, jus' fine, Mr. Wilson. Jus' fine, considerin' my widderhood and how heavy it's weighin' on my heart, what with Sam gone. You know how hard it can be for a widder woman."

"Yes'm, I do. And it pains me mightily to come see you about such a worldly matter when I know your mind is on your late husband and his sojourn in Heaven."

"Mighty nice of you to say so, Mr. Wilson." Lucille moved to the edge of the top step and crossed her ample arms over her ample belly.

Homer knew there'd be no offer of fried chicken or apple pie. He placed his foot on the bottom step. "I only have a minute, Miz Jenkins, but I felt it necessary to discuss payment for Mr. Jenkins's funeral. I know you weren't happy 'bout the way we laid him out, but the bill must be paid. Now, I'm not greedy. I'm a businessman, and I'm here to make a business proposition."

There was a long pause.

Lucille waited.

At last, Homer said, with a straight face, "We're gonna dig Sam up."

Lucille didn't bat an eyelash.

Homer moved in for the kill.

"See now, the casket is ours, so we're willing to take it back. And three months really ain't such long a time so it'll have some resale value. But Sam, he's another matter. And since he belongs to you, we'll bring him back and set him up on your front porch."

Homer's solemn face hid the giggle bubbling up inside.

Lucille feigned shock. Her right hand covered her heart, and her eyes beseeched Heaven. "Mr. Wilson, I know you got to do what you got to do, but have mercy on a poor widder woman. You can't put Sam on the front porch! You can't! Why, that's downright unnatural and un-Christian. What will my neighbors think?"

Homer shrugged and cocked his head. "It's strictly business, Miz Jenkins, strictly business, nothing personal—nothing personal at all. I know you understand."

Lucille's eyes narrowed. She leaned forward and lowered her voice. "Oh, I understand. I understand perfectly. So, tell you what, Homer. You go right ahead and dig Sam up, but have your men take him round back and prop him up next to the garage. My boys'll be home this weekend. We'll figure out what to do with him then."

Homer's mouth dropped open. He was finished. He turned quickly and marched down the walk, slamming the gate behind him.

Lucille shot a "Good day, Homer!" after his retreating back and hummed "Amazing Grace" all the way to the kitchen.

In the end, Lucille never delivered payment, and Homer never delivered Sam.

Waiting for Grace

Reverend Thomas W. Garnett, an ancestor of mine, visited the town where I grew up, decided it would be a good place to live, moved there, and formed a mission that became the Macedonia Baptist Church. This fictional story is based on that fact and on his favorite biblical quotation, "Whoever wants to be great among you will be your servant." (Matthew 20:26)

The feathery black script flowing from the tip of the silver pen ceased with the crossing of a T. Jeremiah S. Garrett sighed, folded the paper, placed it in a long white envelope, and slumped in his seat. He planned to post his letter of resignation as soon as the train pulled into Springfield. The visit with his brother would be a welcome diversion. Then would come another painful decision: what to do with the rest of his life.

Jeremiah was a minister. It was all he'd ever wanted to do, and he would miss it. He was not a Bible thumpin', gospel jumpin', "shout 'em out of hell and into Heaven" kind of preacher. Jeremiah was quiet and serious. He studied the Bible, really studied it. He harvested truth from scripture like farmers harvest wheat from their fields: with purpose, pacing and careful preparation.

Farmers gather sustenance for the body, and Jeremiah was always after sustenance for the soul. He'd select a scripture and let the wind of contemplation winnow chaff from wheat. Then he'd walk with his precious kernels of truth for long miles through the Spotsylvania, Virginia, woods, and only when they were ground fine with reflection would he take them to his pulpit at Mount Olive African Methodist Episcopal (AME) church.

The grounds around the small, whitewashed building were cared for but far from well kept. A few rickety, old steps at the front of the church led to the sanctuary, where the parishioners, mostly as rickety and old as the steps, struggled to keep the church going. It was a losing battle, but Jeremiah was determined to help them in every way he could. This included taking on janitorial duties when necessary.

A few weeks ago, he'd spotted the custodian carrying a broom down the aisle and said, "Brother Scott, let me help you sweep up this morning."

Jeremiah had picked up an extra broom from the vestibule and followed Brother Scott down the aisle. They headed toward the choir loft behind the altar, where the crumbling ceiling had covered the faded red carpet with a fine dusting of white plaster. He watched Brother Scott's slow progress and, placing one hand under his elbow, helped the old man up the altar steps.

Brother Scott smiled his thanks.

Jeremiah looked up. "Seems the patches we put on the ceiling aren't holding up anymore. I'll see about getting a committee together to raise some money. Maybe then we can fix it for good."

"Mighty right of you, Reverend." Brother Scott's withered, balding head bobbed up and down. "Mighty right indeed."

The *swish, swish, swish* of two brooms broke the stillness of the Sunday morning. A crumbling ceiling was the least of

Jeremiah's problems. Every Sunday, Jeremiah preached in his thoughtful, gentle way, and every Sunday, his aging congregation listened patiently, staring at him with bewildered expressions on their faces.

They didn't understand his carefully crafted, heartfelt messages, but they returned every Sunday because their parents had been members of the church. They'd been baptized there. They were loyal and, by God, they would return every week until they died, and then return one last time to be prayed over and put in the ground. But with no new worshippers coming in, Jeremiah's flock was rapidly dwindling. The very existence of Mount Olive was in serious jeopardy.

On the other hand, his neighbor, the Right Reverend J. B. James, was "packin' 'em in." The freshly painted walls of Mount Moriah Baptist Church vibrated each week with the prayers and cries of the devoted. Reverend James was most definitely a Bible thumpin', gospel jumpin', "shout 'em out of hell and into Heaven" kind of preacher.

Jeremiah's church was dying. To save it, he would have to preach fire and brimstone, and this went against his nature. He wasn't sure he could do it, and he wasn't sure he should do it.

He knew he needed to minister. It was his calling. He'd known that since the day he stood in his crib and, filled with a peculiar fire he later understood to be the Holy Spirit, began jabbering to his surprised family as they ate their black-eyed peas and cornbread. With his eyes on the prize, he'd graduated from divinity school at Howard University and returned home to minister to the people who had nurtured and supported him.

Trying to sort his desires from his duties dropped him into a well of grief and confusion. He wondered if Christ had felt something similar during his forty days in the Judean desert.

And then the trees began to burn.

They'd been flaming for weeks. Each time he went into the woods to walk and pray, the trees burst into dazzling tongues of red, gold and orange before his startled eyes. The first time it happened, the evening sun had drenched the green leaves in a glorious rosy light. Then, as he watched in shock, the leaves burst into flames. The trees stood engulfed but were not consumed, and there in the Virginia woods of his childhood, Jeremiah Garrett, the gentle, intellectual man of God, fell to his knees in awe and gratitude, reflecting on Moses and the burning bush. A vision! His first.

With hopeful eyes, he stared into the heart of the flames, looking for an answer. But he saw none. He prayed earnestly, "Dear Lord, it is your words pouring forth through me each Sunday. If I must change, let your spirit shine through me, and I will do your bidding. Amen."

Winter melted into spring. Spring mellowed into summer. The trees continued to burn, and despite prayer, fasting and Bible study, the answer to his dilemma eluded him. He beseeched, "Lord, am I unworthy of your mercy? Must I wander alone through this dark night of my soul? I hunger for your grace. Amen."

Hearing nothing from God, he turned to his sister. Lucille Jenkins had a soft spot for her younger brother and his bookish ways. It wasn't long before Jeremiah found himself sopping up wisdom from her smiling lips as hungrily as he sopped up her chicken gravy with buttermilk biscuits.

"Jeremiah, folk jest don't cotton to your preachin'. You sayin' what Reverend James is sayin', but you sayin' it more genteel and thoughtful-like. Problem is, folk don't want it said serious. They want it more, well, entertainin'. All week, they work they fingers to the bone, strippin' tobacco and cookin' in Miss Ann's kitchen. Come Sunday, they dress up and look to get some soul stretchin', foot stompin', hand clappin' entertainment! Problem is, Jeremiah, you not an entertainer. You a scholar."

She reached across the table and patted his hand. "Your place ain't here, baby brother. You got to fly away and find another nest. Leave."

Leave! Lucille's words thundered down the corridors of his brain. Leave home? Leave the community he'd been a part of all his life? Leave the people who'd raised money to put him through school? Leave Mount Olive? The idea of taking his brand of ministry elsewhere had never occurred to him. *Still,* he thought, *Christ did it. Surely I can do no less. But where should I go? Where am I needed?*

Over the next year, his congregation continued to shrink. Jeremiah wrote letter after letter to every bishop in Virginia, Kentucky, Tennessee and North Carolina. No luck.

When the fire of his faith began to waver, he begged, "Am I to serve you some other way, Lord? Abraham was prepared to give up his firstborn son. Am I to give up the ministry? I am a mere man and find it hard to wait so long on your will. Please, show me a sign. Amen."

The trees blazed. No answer came. His faith withered. Hope faded.

And so, Jeremiah had yielded to the inevitable, and now he sat slumped in his seat as the train rolled on through the New England countryside. He visited his brother every August, but this year, the number of funerals at Mount Olive had delayed his trip by two months.

The letter lay in his lap. The pen dangled from his hand. A sigh of resignation passed his lips. Suddenly, a cheerful voice boomed through the misery in his mind.

"Autumn in New England. A glorious time indeed, don't you think, sir? Your ticket, please."

Jeremiah reached into his coat pocket for the ticket. As he looked up to hand it over, his eyes glanced past the conductor to the window on the other side of the passenger car to see the hills ablaze with red, gold and orange, the brilliant colors of autumn.

His vision! His eyes widened in amazement. His heart stirred. Faith flared anew. Of course! He was to bring his brand of ministry here! He'd been given the sign but hadn't understood its meaning until this minute, this perfect minute overflowing with grace. Amazing!

With profound gratitude, he offered silent thanks and, with wonder in his voice, he brought his gaze back to the conductor. "You know, I don't believe I've ever seen such a glorious, more welcome sight in all my life."

How Sadie Smoked 'Em

Black folks struggled long and hard to gain fair pay, clean working conditions, and the right to unionize in the tobacco industry. This story about a woman who fights to challenge the system highlights a slice of that history.

The abandoned two-story brick building sits on Weston Avenue in Winston-Salem, North Carolina. Nothing bars access. The gate's busted, and the short drive from the entrance reveals thigh-high grass littered with liquor bottles, trash and rusted machinery. The parking lot is empty and wind-blown, filled with abandoned cars and used condoms. Weeds poke their stems and stalks above the broken concrete. The taxi driver's eyes narrow with concern, and he asks if I'm sure this is the place. I say yes. Then he asks, do I want him to wait. I tell him no and watch him drive off through the gate, shaking his head.

I turn to look at the factory. In the jagged, glass shards of the broken windows, I see a woman who listened when the voice in her head said, "Leave the heels in the suitcase and wear sneakers."

Trash crunches under my feet as I take a few steps forward before stopping at the front door that hangs lopsided from its hinges. The wind blows the door back and forth with a creaking, moaning, mournful melody. Fire has blackened most of the still-visible brick facade. Kudzu vine hides the rest, winding itself around the building like a boa constrictor seeking to kill and feed off its prey.

This image, along with my memories of the place, sends a shiver up my spine. I'm here because the Winston-Salem Historical Society plans to turn the factory into a museum. Imagine that!

The director of community engagement, Deborah Grover, called me last month. She said the society would pay to fly me down from New York and put me up in a hotel. They want to interview me and take pictures before the renovation starts. They plan to put up a plaque with my name, Sadie Mae Thompson, on the wall next to the entrance. If I'm still vertical, ventilating and on the right side of the ground when the museum is ready to open, they want to honor me at the dedication ceremony. Lawdy me!

The story, and my part in it, began when my family migrated from the backwoods of Kentucky to Winston-Salem, looking for work and a better life. We found a small measure of relief from the bitter racism of the Deep South, but the subtle racism of "Up South" confused us no end. We did not find a better life, but we did find work. The tobacco industry was booming. I began working part-time at Smith & Rhodes Tobacco Company in 1934, when I was fourteen, and then started working full time in 1940.

You'd think with all the tobacco around, it would've been easy for me to pick up a cigarette and fall into the smoking habit, but I never did. One day in that place was enough to turn me off anything with tobacco in it. The work was dirty and the hours were long, but the pay, although low, was steady. And I much preferred working at the factory to cooking and cleaning for the wealthy White women who lived nearby on "the hill."

It was mostly Black women working on the factory floor and running the machines 'cause the men were off fighting the Japanese and the Germans. The White women worked upstairs, assembling and packing. They wore clean white uniforms while we did grunt work in whatever we'd worn from home.

It was hard work and dirty. First, the cured tobacco would come in. Some of us would strip leaves from the stalks, and others would sort it into grades. It was nasty, dusty, hot, smelly and dangerous. Some of the women fainted, got tuberculosis, or miscarried from the toxic atmosphere in the rooms. And we were constantly vomiting from the fumes. We tried wearing handkerchiefs over our noses and mouths to avoid breathing in the nauseating tobacco dust. Later, Blanche Jackson came up with the trick of putting orange segments in our mouths to keep from throwing up. Open windows would have helped, but the floor manager kept them tightly shut.

If that wasn't enough, we had to put up with verbal abuse and what they now call "sexual harassment" from the foremen and managers. What we called it was low-down behavior from triflin' men. Worst was when one of them would take one of us to the office for an hour or more. We knew what was going on, but had no way to stop it, no how. And none of us talked about it to each other. We were too ashamed.

Yeah, working conditions were bad, but they were bad everywhere if you were Black, especially if you were Black and female. So we figured we might as well make the most money we could. We were definitely a bunch of angry Black women. Nowadays, the label "angry Black woman" is a stereotype, but back then it was too true. The time came when me and my sister coworkers got fed up and kicked much corporate ass. It's amazing what you can do when you stick together.

It started one Sunday afternoon in May 1943 after the potluck at church. Potlucks were a regular thing. Everybody brought a dish, and the whole congregation would share Sunday dinner.

The folks who brought food were the first in line to wrap up leftovers for their families. That afternoon, I suggested all us factory workers sit together and see if we could figure out how to handle what we faced on the job without getting fired.

I did it because of an article I read in *The Beacon*, the local Black newspaper. It was an editorial written by the owner, Brewster Bennett, and it was about something called a "union." None of us knew what that really meant or how one article could change everything, but we were catching so much hell we needed to do something to change our working conditions. After all, we couldn't afford to quit. We were fired up!

We started meeting every Friday night after work. One night, we'd meet at Ida's house, the next at Lulu's and... Well, you get the idea.

It took us six months to read everything we could get our hands on about slowdowns, strikes and forming a union. We invited Brewster to our meetings, and one night he brought in a tall, skinny White man. Of course, we froze up and got real quiet, but Brewster said Fred Goldberg was a trusted friend who planned to show us how to do what they called "civil rights labor organizing."

Those were fancy words, but if those words and what they stood for could help us get clean, safe working conditions, we were willing to do whatever was necessary. Fred planned to teach us strategies and techniques to be successful. It would be hard and scary, he said. It would take a long time, but if we were determined, he would be there to help. We listened. We talked. We organized and got all but a few Black folk involved.

Brewster and Fred brought in a few race men; folks who'd dedicated their lives to the uplift of Black folk. They trained us in what to say, when to say it, how to say it, and who to say it to. We drew up our demands. And when we were done, the committee elected me president. Me!

I can tell you, the only thing keeping me steady and standing my ground during those times was my cousin Lucille. She is a determined, fearless woman who takes no shit from anyone. Brewster was kind enough to let me use his phone, and I called Lucille every time my courage weakened. She'd boost me up, and I'd redouble my efforts to live up to the trust my coworkers put in me.

At last, I was ready. I delivered our demands in person to Mr. Rhodes with Brewster at my side. Fred stayed in the background, said his presence would just bring trouble. Rhodes was civil. He took the papers and assured us he would get back to us in two weeks. But you know he didn't. Three weeks later, after a planning meeting with Brewster and Fred, we went on strike at exactly 12:10 p.m. on a Wednesday afternoon.

That's when the lunch whistle blew and all of us Black folk, near three hundred women and men, left our workstations and walked out of the factory to gather in the yard, where we all stood with our backs to the building.

Lawd, you shoulda heard the managers bellow and threaten to fire us when we refused to go back in after lunchtime. But we knew they wouldn't. Without us doing our work, the White folks couldn't do theirs. They needed us and now we knew it too.

Rhodes sent out the vice president to promise they'd look into our complaints if we'd just go back to work. I gave the signal, and we all sang "We Shall Not Be Moved" to drown him out. And we stayed out on strike.

The factory bosses tried hiring strikebreakers, most of them White, but they couldn't stomach the work and quit after a few days.

It took months to resolve. We got a lot of abuse and pushback along the way. It was more "Up South" difficult than Deep South dangerous, but it was still a lot.

The tight-knit group of factory bigwigs, small business owners, and local politicians who lived on "the hill" saw our movement as a threat. They came up with a strong-arm tactic to intimidate us and drive a wedge between us. First, they tried to fire the Black women who worked as maids and nannies for the wives of these men, the women we called "Miss Ann." The meanness of that threat rolled down the hill toward us like a boulder set to crush our spirits until Miss Ann put down her high-heeled foot and became an unwitting ally. In no way were those women going to give up their card games, clubs and high society teas to take care of their kids, cook supper, do laundry, or clean their own toilets.

Then, the men who owned the property and the houses we lived in tried to evict us when we couldn't pay rent. That fell flat because Brewster, Fred and the race men went around the country raising money to cover our rent so we could continue to fight. The churches and Black businesses came together to make sure we were fed, kept safe from threats, and had a place to meet.

Next, Brewster and Fred spread our story to the big newspapers. We got a nice break when workers at other tobacco factories in the city and surrounding areas followed our lead to demand better working conditions for themselves. The tobacco industry ground to a halt, first in Winston-Salem and then across the whole state. That brought Rhodes to the negotiation table. Well, that and the fact that it was wartime and the soldiers off fighting in Europe and the Far East needed their cigarettes.

The two tables we set up in the basement at AME Zion faced each other, but several feet of space separated them like a symbol for how Black and White people lived their lives back then. I knew the training I'd gotten and the meetings I'd organized and chaired would stand me in good stead for what was to come.

Despite last night's phone call to Lucille, I was nervous as a mouse being hunted by a hungry cat. My stomach was tied in knots, my skin itched, and my mind hopped on the anger-fear roller coaster I'd been riding for months. I took my seat and waited.

A few minutes later, Rhodes and his lawyers walked in and looked around disapprovingly before taking their seats across from me. With Brewster on my left, Fred and our lawyers on my right, and a few of my closest sister-friends flanking them, I did what I was trained to do. I took a deep breath in, exhaled and called the meeting to order.

The meetings happened every other day for three weeks before we came to a temporary compromise. We agreed to work four hours a day at our regular pay until the two sides negotiated an agreement. We did that so the soldiers fighting overseas would get their smokes.

Of course, Rhodes balked, yelled and refused to sign the final document, which met most of our demands and aligned with federal labor laws. But by this time the mayor and city council were fed up. The marches, the reporters, the bad press, and the disruption to tourism and business were having a devastating effect on the local economy. Those folk took the pressure hose off us and turned it toward Rhodes and the executives at the other tobacco factories in the county.

One week later, Rhodes gave in. The union movement sweeping the country had finally reached the Black folks of Winston-Salem, North Carolina. We got our union, better pay and, most important, better working conditions, including open windows and grudging respect for our humanity from the managers. By this time, we even had a few White folks joining us when they realized what we were fighting for would benefit them too.

That was sixty years ago. Since then, life's been quiet. I married, moved north, raised my children, spoiled my grandchildren, and now here I am. Isn't it funny? I never smoked cigarettes while working at Smith & Rhodes, but the girls and me? Ha! We sure did smoke the company!

The sound of a car driving up snaps me back to the present. I turn to see a Volkswagen pull up and park. A small White woman gets out, waves and introduces herself as Deborah Grover.

Seems like my life and the life of this building have come together full circle, and I'm gonna get my fifteen minutes of fame. Lawdy me. Will wonders never cease?

The Lady in Red

When the body of a woman in a glass coffin is discovered on the property of Larry and Marilyn Winston, the investigation into her identity and how she came to be placed in a secret room on the Barrington estate reveals surprising and complicated connections between the current and former owners.

Larry and Marilyn Winston, the new owners of Barrington Hall, are waiting for me on the front steps of their nineteenth-century mansion. Four massive pillars rise from the wraparound porch to support the second-story balcony. Tall, evenly spaced windows, their tiny panes eerily resembling eyes, peer nervously over the railing. They are not the only evidence of anxiety at Barrington Hall this morning.

Larry keeps wiping sweat off his forehead with a white handkerchief. Marilyn's left hand taps her thigh, producing tiny ripples in the fabric of her beige cotton skirt. As a forensic genealogist, my job is to pay attention to the details, which can tell you a lot. And those two details tell me that Larry and Marilyn are disturbed.

They usher me into their cozy, wood-paneled den and serve me cold lemonade—a welcome drink on a hot summer's day.

After a few minutes of obligatory social chitchat about their health and the weather, they get down to the business of why they've summoned me here.

"Della, I've always loved this house." Marilyn leans forward, her lips smiling and her eyes softening. "It's funny, you know. As a kid, I used to ride by on my bike. I could feel the house's energy. It pulled at me in a way I didn't and still don't understand. Anyway, when it came time for us to buy a house"—her eyes slide sideways, toward her husband—"I'll admit I pushed Larry a bit. We got my dream house, but it's turning into a nightmare." She sits back and exhales. Her left hand again starts tapping at her thigh.

"We found the body in the outbuilding." Larry wipes more sweat from his forehead.

You may think the next words out of my mouth should have been, "Why didn't you call the police?" They weren't because this particular body had been dead since 1850. Let me explain.

Since the 1600s, Barrington Hall had belonged to the Barrington family. The family's fortunes stemmed from cotton production built on the backs of enslaved people, only to evaporate after the Civil War. They held on to the property as long as they could, but last year, finances had forced the oldest remaining Barringtons, Basil and Meredith, to sell the house with its outbuilding to the Winstons. The sale must have seemed ironic to the Barringtons because Larry and Marilyn Winston are card-carrying members of the Black upper class.

Like any proud new property owners, Larry and Marilyn set about making the house their home. After major renovations to the kitchen and bathrooms in the Big House, Marilyn turned her attention to the small brick outbuilding with the columned facade. In the 1880s, the building had served as an office. Now fallen into disuse and disrepair, it had become a storage shed for five generations of belongings and knickknacks that were no longer needed or wanted.

A month ago, Marilyn decided to turn it into a recreation space where their two teenagers could host hangout sessions and parties for their friends. So the home improvement crew had begun clearing out what the Barringtons had left behind. A familiar routine of rip, sort and salvage unfolded over the next few weeks until they pulled down a heavy tapestry on the back wall and discovered a door sealed with a large, ornate metal lock. Marilyn told them to take the door off its hinges, salvage the wood and save the lock, which could've been a valuable antique. When they removed the door, they discovered the mystery—and the next day, they hired me to solve it.

A few minutes after our meeting, I walked into the room to see four wood-paneled walls dotted with narrow shelves. On them stood candlesticks and candelabras with half-burned beeswax candles. On a low table in the middle of the room lies the body of a young Black woman in a glass-lidded iron coffin. She may have been beautiful, but the ugly, crusted smallpox lesions covering her face make it impossible to tell.

Presumably, the body isn't decomposed because the coffin was filled with preservative alcohol and sealed. She looks as if she died only a few days ago. She's wearing a long-sleeved red silk dress with a white lace collar. White gloves hide her hands, and square-toed black boots peek out from a full, dome-shaped skirt. Her hair, parted in the center, lies flat against her scalp, and her head rests on a now discolored embroidered pillow. An engraved plaque on the side of the coffin reads:

MY DEAREST A., I WILL LOVE YOU FOREVER, C. 1850

I warn Marilyn and Larry to stop work on the outbuilding and lock it up. Then I head off to city hall.

"Morning, Della." Steve Pawlski, the town clerk, greets me with his usual easygoing smile. We're professional friends. In my line of work, keepers of records, like deeds and genealogical information, are the keys to success. I treat them well, remember their kids' birthdays, ask about their health, and patiently listen as they tell me about their promotion, their anniversary, or what their spouse or partner gave them for Christmas, Hanukah or Kwanzaa.

"Back atcha, Steve. Today I need to see birth, death and ownership records relating to the Barrington place from 1800 to 1900."

He waves me over to the microfiche machine. I settle in, and a few minutes later Steve brings over a box labeled "19th-Century Barrington Family." I start with the birth and death records to see how many "C's" were alive in the mid-1800s.

I check both male and female names. I have to rule out all possibilities. It's important not to overlook any detail in my line of work. Could C have been a woman? It's highly unlikely, but certainly possible. If a female "C" loved "A" in the mid-1800s, I doubt she'd have had the money or authority to build a secret room and preserve a body with such style and care, especially a Black body. And indeed, I found no female names beginning with "C."

The list of male names consists of one Cecil and two Caesars. The next task is to check ownership records because only the official landowner would have been able to arrange this strange resting place for the body of the woman he loved. At the time, relationships between White men and Black women, owner and enslaved, were either secret or forced. Given the nature of those relationships, I could assume nothing about A's feelings for C based on the evidence so far.

The list of owners includes Abraham Barrington, 1820–1845; Cecil Barrington, 1845–1879; and Jeremiah Barrington, 1879–1908. I've found C. Now I need to find A.

Basil and Meredith Barrington gasp out their "oh no's" and "oh my Gods" as I tell them about the body of the Black woman hidden on their former property. However, I can see curiosity beginning to emerge from under the cover of their genteel southern manner.

After a few more sips of sweet tea and some polite conversation, I learn they know nothing of any family story about the mystery woman, who she was, or how she came to be laid to rest, so elegantly dressed, in a glass coffin.

"Do you have any family documents or records on slave holdings?" I ask. "Would they be somewhere in the office where the body was found?"

Basil shakes his head, the fingers of his right hand tapping his khaki-covered thigh. "You can look, but I doubt you'll find anything. Grandpa was the last Barrington to use the outbuilding. It was a private drinking club for him and his buddies. The only things we've ever found there were drawers and shelves filled with empty bourbon bottles."

My exhaustive search of the old plantation office proves Basil correct. My next stop will be a search of Federal Census records at the National Archives in Washington, DC. It won't be easy or quick. The letter "A" is not going to get me far, and enslaved folks rarely had surnames. The one helpful detail I have is the name of the plantation owner and the approximate period in which to search. I am sure the Barringtons kept good household records. If the family didn't destroy them and they survived the burning of the local courthouse during the Civil War, they would have been turned over to the Census Bureau.

A few days later, I dig into the census records for the Barrington plantation and find three enslaved female "A's" during the early to mid-1800s. The most likely "A" is a woman named Arabella. In 1830, the Barringtons purchased her along with her mother. She was five years old. On November 15, 1848, at the age of eighteen, Arabella gave birth to a baby boy named Cecil. There was no record of his being sold or of his death. Where did he go?

I have a sneaking hunch and ask Basil if he has the family Bible from the mid-1800s. He does. At his dining room table, wearing white cotton gloves to protect the ancient pages, I turn to the family birth and death records—and there he is. Cecil Barrington II, born November 15, 1848. Father listed as Cecil Barrington. Mother's name not recorded. The rest of the entries note Cecil II's graduation from Yale University, his marriage to a schoolteacher named Anna Turner, the births of their three children, George, Arabella and James, and the date of his death. There is no more information about his life or why he did not inherit the property after his father's death, although any thinking person today who understands southern history can make an educated guess.

It looks to me that, willing or not, "A" is the enslaved mother of Cecil II. Cecil Senior acknowledged his birth, raised him as White and found a way to honor the woman he loved and to grieve her death from smallpox.

This is what I live for—solving family mysteries. Next, I ask Basil if he would be willing to take a DNA test. Since the Winstons grew up in town, I ask them too. They want to know why. I tell them I'm checking out a long shot.

The results come in a few weeks later, confirming my hunch. Basil Barrington has African ancestry in his family bloodline.

I give the Barringtons the news seated on a floral chintz sofa in the living room of their condominium. Meredith gasps and clutches her pearls. Basil nods. "I was afraid it might be something like this," he says with an air of resignation. "Given my family's slave-owning history, it's not much of a surprise. Of course"—he pauses and glances over at Meredith, who is attempting to wipe the look of horror from her face—"It's not something most folks freely admit or talk about. Still, it's our history and our reality, whether we like it or not."

What I tell them next leaves Basil wide-eyed and speechless. Meredith runs sobbing from the room. I ask Basil if he wants to go after her. He shakes his head. "She'll be okay. I'll talk to her after she cries it out." He sits back. "I'm going to have to think about this. It's a lot for us to handle, and we have to get ourselves together before we tell our children and grandchildren."

I have one more visit to make. It's late afternoon by the time I'm sitting in the Winstons' den. Larry makes us drinks—mine is a vodka tonic. I take a sip and give them the news. Their surprise gives way to rippling laughter from Marilyn and a grin from Larry.

Basil Barrington and Marilyn Winston share a common ancestor. Is it "A?" Or did another Barrington cross the color line to father mixed-race children? Is this the source of Marilyn's lifelong fascination with Barrington Hall?

Marilyn wants to know where my long-shot hunch came from. "Details," I tell her—small things others might overlook. In this case, it's the way both she and Basil tap their thighs when nervous or anxious. I'd seen the two of them do it often over the weeks of research and meetings. Small details scream, if you can hear them.

A fortnight later, Marilyn and Larry make arrangements for a tasteful and touching funeral service for "A." Basil, Meredith and I are invited to sit next to Marilyn and Larry. Meredith displays "a stiff upper lip," as the saying goes. As the service begins, I watch Basil lean over to Marilyn and whisper, "It's strange to think I sold my ancestral home to someone I'm related to." He smiles. "But it's good to know it's still in the family."

Later, at Memorial Park Cemetery, I stand by the two couples and watch the glass coffin being lowered to its final resting place. Like I said, I live for solving family mysteries. But despite my best efforts, our lady in red is taking the answer to this one to her grave.

Mama Rose's Kitchen

A New York reporter covers a story about the Georgia voter suppression laws of 2021 and discovers how history, family and politics intersect in the small town of Barrington, Georgia.

The first time I saw Maybelle Rose Cartwright, she was standing on the steps of the county courthouse in Barrington, Georgia. The skirt on her blue, flowered dress and the matching ribbon on her wide-brimmed church hat fluttered gently in the spring breeze. I watched her standing there, her eyes directed skyward. I imagined she was savoring victory and thanking God for the ability to remain steadfast and resilient through the storm descending on her, the town and, dare I say it, the country. As a reporter, I was here to cover her story.

In symbolic ways, Maybelle resembles David, the young shepherd boy who toppled the giant Goliath and saved Israel. But that's where the resemblance ends. Maybelle, sixty-two years young, is almost a giant herself, six feet tall with fierce, snapping eyes set to bore through you like a laser through steel. The sheep she cares for are the people who show up every day at Mama Rose's Kitchen, where she serves them fried chicken, corn pudding, potato salad, collard greens, Hoppin' John—black-eyed peas and rice cooked with smoked ham hocks—and buttermilk biscuits. I could go on and list her entire menu, but my mouth waters way too much when I think about it. And since I want to tell you the whole story, I'm going to cut it short at the buttermilk biscuits.

Maybelle's story is epic. It dominated the news in Fulton County for weeks, and even got picked up by the national cable news stations.

Knowing I'd be interrupting her thoughts, but also knowing I had to if I was going to beat out the competition gathered behind me, I took the steps two at a time.

"Ms. Cartwright? Ms. Cartwright! May I have a few moments of your time?"

She lowered her gaze from the sky to take me in, then raised it higher to take in the others moving up the steps behind me, shouting their own questions. She looked back at me and quietly asked, "What do y'all want with me?"

She seemed genuinely puzzled. I smiled to myself and said, "Ms. Carter, what happened here in Barrington is all over the news. People want to hear your story from the beginning."

I jabbed a thumb toward the gaggle of reporters, cameras and lights behind me. "All of us want to help them hear it, but I'll give you as much time as you need to think about it and keep the rest of these people out of your hair, if you let me be the one to write it up."

A slow smile spread over her copper-colored face. She tipped her head to the right, held her hat in place with her hand, and said, "Come see me tomorrow, young man. Do you know where my place is?"

I knew. Everyone following the story knew. Ms. Maybelle runs Mama Rose's Kitchen on Holden Street. "Yes, ma'am. I know. What time should I come?"

"Three o'clock, between dinner and supper. I'll be free then."

I nodded, cleared a path for her through the others, and kept them at bay as she lowered herself into the car that whisked her away.

The next day, I turned right off Magnolia Avenue onto Holden Street. The houses looked as though they'd sheltered generations of folk in this mostly Black working- and middle-class neighborhood. The old-growth maple trees on many of the front lawns sprouted spring leaves that would eventually provide welcome summer shade. Despite their age, the collection of single-family homes and duplexes were well cared for—the sidewalks and street, filled with cracks and frost heaves from the winter, not so much. It was clear the city hadn't kept up its end of the bargain.

Ms. Maybelle's two-story house was at the end of the street. Its bright yellow paint presented a stark contrast to the green shutters and the windows trimmed in dark red. I parked, got out and walked past the small front yard up three cement steps. They led to a wide wraparound screen porch sporting six small tables, each surrounded by four wicker chairs. The tables were topped with crisp red-and-white checkered tablecloths. A hand-lettered sign above the front door read:

MAMA ROSE'S KITCHEN
COME ON IN AND SET A SPELL

The door was slightly ajar, allowing smells from the kitchen to waft onto the porch. I took a whiff and thought, *Breaking news! Supper will be amazing!* My northern nose couldn't separate the aromas into their component parts, but the headline made my stomach growl. If the interview went well, I would stay and research supper firsthand.

A cheery "Come on in!" answered my knock. I pushed the door open and stepped in to see Ms. Maybelle busing tables, scooping up the lunch dishes and silverware, and placing them on a small cart. She wiped her hands on her apron and waved me toward the bar at the back of the room. "Sit yourself down, young man, I'll be with you as soon as I finish cleaning off the tables."

I could see the entire front of the house from my barstool. Ms. Maybelle and her husband had turned it into a restaurant. But how? This was a residential neighborhood. Getting the answer to this question would be my first task.

"Can I get you something to drink?"

I turned back and found myself staring at a short, round man who looked like a tanned, ponytailed Santa Claus. "I'm Elliot, Maybelle's husband, partner, all-around handyman and, most recently, bartender. What's your pleasure?"

"Got any Guinness?"

"Bottle or draft?"

"Bottle. Thanks."

Elliot's eyes twinkled. His hands popped the cap and poured the stout into a tall glass with the perfect amount of foam on top. He placed it on a cardboard coaster in front of me and smiled. "I'm glad you're going to tell Maybelle's story. I've been talking to her 'bout it, but she can be stubborn and thick-headed." He shook his head and laughed. "But she's mostly always right!"

"Well, I hope she'll decide to trust me to do right by her."

We shook hands. "'Scuse me now. I got to go clean the grill." Elliot went out through the door at the end of the bar and left me with my Guinness and my thoughts.

A few minutes later, Ms. Maybelle came in with two tall glasses of lemonade and suggested we sit outside with them and talk.

I left my empty beer glass on the bar and followed her to the porch.

"So," she said once we'd taken our seats, "what do you want to ask me?"

"Well, Ms. Maybelle, my first question is, how can you operate a restaurant and bar in a residential neighborhood?"

She chuckled. "It's a long story. Here's the short version. My Grandma Rose began feeding folk from the front porch during the Depression. My mom kept up the tradition when things got better. Soon, folks started leaving money on the tables. So, she made up a menu, painted the sign over the door, and started serving supper two nights during the week, plus Sunday dinner after church. After Momma passed, Elliot and I turned the front of the homestead into a regular restaurant and expanded it to serving meals every day but Monday. Now Mama Rose's Kitchen pays the bills and supports three of our four children in college." She swept her arms around to take in the porch, the house and the yard. "And here we are."

"But Ms. Maybelle, what about the permits and the liquor license?"

Her chuckle turned into a belly laugh. "Oh, right... You're from up north. New York would be my guess. Am I right?"

"Yes, ma'am."

Ms. Maybelle sat back, crossed her long, elegant legs, and gave this Yankee a quick lesson on how things work in Barrington. Turns out the town got its name from the Barrington family, who owned the land in the 1600s and operated the area's largest cotton plantation. Maybelle's ancestors were enslaved there. After the Civil War, they worked as sharecroppers, housemaids and mammies for the Barrington family.

"Today," she said, "the Barringtons run the town. They leave us alone. We leave them alone. The town has always turned a blind eye to what we do. I think they see it as some form of reparation. It's how things are." She paused, shook her head and added, "Or were until last year."

Feet pounding up the steps caught our attention, and Maybelle looked past me to the door. Her eyes opened wide, then narrowed into slits. I turned to see a large, red-faced White man in a beige suit and straw Panama hat open the screen door, step in and stop when he saw me.

"Afternoon, Maybelle."

"Good afternoon," she said. I noticed she did not say his name.

The man took off his hat, cleared his throat, and in what appeared to be a conciliatory tone, said, "I... I... I was hoping to catch you alone." He looked me over from head to toe before turning back to Ms. Maybelle. She had not moved an inch.

"What do you want?" she asked flatly.

"I'm hoping we can let bygones be bygones. It was nothing personal. You gotta know that, Maybelle."

Ms. Maybelle did not move or respond in any way.

"C'mon, Maybelle. This is me! You know me. You know I don't have nothin' against you or the others. I was just doin' my job."

I watched Maybelle Rose Cartwright jump out of her chair, storm over to the man, and stab a finger in his face. In a barely controlled voice, she said, "Wyatt Maynard Barrington, if you learn nothing else in this life, know this. In this town, with our history, everything political is personal. It's not an either/or thing. It's a both/and. I'm a walking, talking example. And by God, you'd better remember that before you come anywhere near me in the future. Do. You. Understand?" she asked, accentuating each word with another jab of her finger.

"Aww, Maybelle..."

He started to say something else but then glanced at me and thought better of it. Instead, he clapped his hat on his head, turned and left.

I smelled a twist in the story. "Who is he, Ms. Maybelle?"

"He's my cousin, a bunch of times removed. And he's the sheriff. He wrote up the charge and arrested me last fall."

"Your cousin! B-But..."

"Don't look so surprised, young man. It's another way things work around here. It's not the first time or the last his family and mine got together one way or another, and like it or not, we're related. Hell's bells, if truth be told, half the Black folk in this town are related to half the White folk in this town. It's what you might call an open secret, even if most folks don't like to admit it or talk about it."

Maybelle laughed at the bewildered expression on my face. "Why, just last year my niece called to tell me we're related to another branch of the Caucasian family tree through a Barrington named Basil. Pah! I can't keep track."

She waved her hand back and forth as her next words brought us once more to the matter under discussion. "Anyway, until Wyatt arrested me, he would show up on weekdays for supper and a drink after work, and on Sundays, he'd be here for breakfast before church and dinner after. He's the main reason Elliot and I don't worry about permits or a liquor license. It's a family thing, or at least it was."

My research covered all aspects of southern history, but it's one thing to read about it in a book and quite another to see it play out in front of your eyes in the middle of a political freak storm. I could think of only one thing to ask her next. "Are you sorry about what happened?"

Ms. Maybelle sat back down in her chair, sighed and stared up at the wooden ceiling with the same expression she'd borne yesterday on the courthouse steps. After a moment, she lowered her head and looked at me. "No, young man, absolutely not. I'd do it all over again." She paused and placed a hand on her heart. "Yes, indeed, I most certainly would do it all over again."

Elliot's head popped around the open front door. "Heard a ruckus. Everything all right out here, Maybelle?"

"Yes, hon. He showed up, just like we figured. I sent him packin'."

Elliot looked worried. "Now, sweetie, don't you think...?"

Ms. Maybelle lifted the hand from her heart and waved away Elliot's words as though she were batting a pesky mosquito. "I know. I know. It'll take a bit of time, but it'll be all right in the end."

Elliot still looked worried, but he said "okay" and went back inside.

Ms. Maybelle turned to me. "Young man, what *is* your name? I can't sit here and call you 'young man' all afternoon."

"It's Brian. Brian Albright. I'm a freelancer for the *New Yorker.* I write articles on current affairs and social issues."

Ms. Maybelle's eyebrows lifted. Her head tilted to the right. "Writing pays your bills?"

"Yes, ma'am. I make a good living writing about current affairs, and I never run out of material."

She chuckled again, a pleasant sound I could listen to for hours. "Sounds about right. Where you find folks, you find affairs of all kinds and plenty of issues to go along with 'em." She slapped the table with one hand and leaned forward. "So, what do you want to know? We need to be done soon, Brian. I've got to get supper ready. Can't keep hungry folk waiting."

"Would it be okay if I record our conversation? I want your words in your voice. I want your story to come through, not my interpretation of what I hear." I held my breath as I waited for her answer.

Her eyes seemed to stare right through me for a moment, then she nodded. I reached into my backpack, pulled out my phone, and set it to voice record.

"Now, Ms. Maybelle, tell me how all this started."

She took a sip of her lemonade. "The latest chapter in our town's long, complicated story began last spring, when the governor signed a new voter suppression bill into law. All the legal details and wording are complicated, but the part that set my teeth on edge said it is now illegal to give food and water to folks standing in line to vote. My blood boils just to think about it!

"My lawyer, Billie Ray, Elliot's nephew, schooled me in the letter of the law. It was meant to prevent what they call 'line warming,' a way to persuade folks in line to vote one way or the other. It used to be just signs, speeches or written material that wasn't allowed. But now, it means food and water too." She pressed her lips tight and shook her head.

"Did you break the law?" I asked.

"Course not!" she snorted. "The letter of the law is clear as a bell. My problem was and is with the spirit behind it."

Now we were getting to the heart of the matter, a complicated one not covered well by either side of the news divide. I call what I do 'walking the grays.' I try to understand the complexity of human motives behind stories because thirty-second sound bites and catchy slogans can't. I was after the truth, and I knew Ms. Maybelle could give it to me.

"What do you mean by 'the spirit of the law'?" I asked.

"Brian, the spirit of the law is meant to make it harder for us to vote. The White folk are scared if we get power, we'll do to them like they've done to us. So they close polling places and limit hours to those still standing. It means long lines on the few weekends when the polls are open. Those lines wrap around the block, making folks stand and wait for hours to do their civic duty. It's enough to shame the devil, or it oughta be! My family's been feeding and helping folks for generations, so it was a no-brainer for Elliot and me to find ways around both the letter and spirit of the law to help folks."

"What did you do?"

"We got volunteers from churches, PTAs and community groups to pack brown bags with water, a sandwich, cookies and a snack. We got umbrellas donated in case of hot sun or rain. We told volunteers to wear clothes with no political symbols or words on them. We measured the distance from the polling places so we knew where to set up our tables. Each table had a sign saying:

Free Food and Water Please Take A Bag

Then we stood twenty-five feet away from the tables so we wouldn't get near any voter walking up to a table to grab a bag. We set up tables at every polling place in town."

"Did you include predominately White areas?"

Ms. Maybelle gave a hearty laugh. "You know it. Our volunteers looked like the United Nations. We weren't going to be accused of favoring one group over another. We documented the whole thing with pictures, videos, interviews with volunteers and with voters after they voted."

They had indeed covered all their bases and followed the letter of the law. I took a sip of my drink. "Seems to me, you took your political lemons and made lemonade."

Ms. Maybelle didn't miss a beat. "Indeed we did, son. Indeed we did."

"Now Ms. Maybelle, if you followed the letter of the law, why did Sheriff Wyatt's arrest statement charge you for violating it?"

She smiled, and I could tell there was another lesson coming my way about how things worked in the South.

"Oh, he didn't arrest me on the letter of the law. He arrested me, handcuffed me, stuffed me into one of his damn patrol cars, and hauled me off to jail because of the spirit of the law. In the minds of the White folks, I violated the spirit of the law and around these parts, that's enough to get you into a heap of trouble."

"Surely, he must have known it wouldn't stand up in court."

"Oh, he knew. And he'd never have done this on his own. He was pressured from the top. What I'm angry about—but not surprised at—is that he didn't push back. Based on our history, this is the way things have worked here since before we were babies. He buckled under the pressure. The goal was to put a monkey wrench into any plan defying the spirit of the law. In the North, y'all have a saying: 'driving while Black' or 'DWB.' Down here, it's 'VWB,' '*voting* while Black.' And family or not, Wyatt's a damn coward!"

"Seeing as how he's your cousin and you have a long history together, won't this leave a big hole in your life and that of your restaurant if it can't be fixed? Are you going to be able to mend things with him?"

"I'm working on forgiveness because I'm a Christian, but it's not easy. In his heart, Wyatt loves me like family. He says it all the time. In his mind, although he'll never admit it, he thinks he's better than me because he's White. His mind, not his heart, still dictates what his behind does. His love is based on me staying in my place, as defined by him and his kind. Since my arrest, I've met more people of goodwill—Black, White and every shade in between. They've filled up all the empty spaces in my love bank left by Wyatt's sorry-ass withdrawals." She stopped then and said, "Oh, my… That wasn't kind. My apologies. Please don't print that."

In the end, I didn't. We talked for another forty-five minutes or so, and then I stayed for a supper of BBQ, potato salad, collard greens, biscuits and sweet tea. After stuffing my face and my stomach, I said goodbye to the Cartwrights, along with the typical sentiments about keeping in touch and visiting again.

What I did do, after I wrote the story, was send Ms. Maybelle a draft copy. That went against journalistic protocol, but I needed Ms. Maybelle's approval more than I wanted to please my editor or garner glowing reviews. Thankfully, she was happy with it.

The next year, I took another trip south to follow up on the story. A lot had changed. Georgia had elected its first woman governor, who happens to be Black. She's working with the new legislature to overhaul the state's voting laws. I went back to Mama Rose's Kitchen to get Ms. Maybelle's take on the changes.

When I got there, the porch and dining room were jam-packed with people and the air buzzed with excitement. I managed to make my way to the bar to greet Elliot and order a drink. On my way out, I saw a makeshift stage, podium and microphone at one end of the porch. At the other end, I found Ms. Maybelle chatting with a group of people. She spotted me, came over to give me a hug, and answered my question before I could even open my mouth to ask it. "Brian, honey, welcome back. Now, you go find yourself a seat and have supper. Come back tomorrow for dinner and we'll talk then—got no time tonight." She smiled, waved and disappeared into the crowd, while I sat, ate and listened to the evening's program and speeches.

The next day, Ms. Maybelle, Elliot and I sat down for the midday meal I call "lunch" and dyed-in-the-wool southerners call "dinner." Last night's event had been a celebration to welcome Ms. Maybelle Cartwright to the Barrington City Council for a two-year term.

After the dust had settled from her political activism and court case, the good people of Barrington encouraged her to run for city council. After some hesitation, a firm nudge from her voter rights volunteers—plus a gentle push from Elliot—convinced her to run. And she won. Wyatt, meanwhile, lost his bid for another term as sheriff.

She and Wyatt have tentatively reconciled. He's back at Mama Rose's Kitchen, eating supper every night, breakfast before church on Sunday and dinner after.

Looks to me like Ms. Maybelle's food, more than anything else, is the glue reuniting them, despite history, politics, race and personal differences. Ms. Maybelle is hoping his gut and heart will eventually change his mind and his behind, but she's not holding her breath.

The Lateral Drift of Mariposa Jones

It's the 1990s, and Mariposa learns to stop "shoulding" on herself. In the process, she finds clarity and the courage to follow her dream.

Mariposa stared through the kitchen window at her spring-green lawn and tree-lined street. Her throat tightened. She choked back tears. "Damn! Here it comes again."

She slammed her fist against the granite counter, surprised that the gold Formica flecks didn't scatter onto the floor from the force of the blow. She lifted her head, opened her mouth, and screamed at the top of her lungs, "Damn it to hell! What am I supposed to do?"

"It" came from the space where her uterus and ovaries used to be, a somber shadow rising hungrily to suck the joie de vivre from her life of domestic and professional perfection. Tears bullied their way past her steely control and marched down her cheeks. There was simply too much to do and too many people depending on her to do it—two teenagers, a husband, students, parents, a principal and a dog.

"There's no time for me," she sobbed, "and if there were, I don't know what I'd do with it!"

Wiping her eyes, she trudged to the bedroom, touched up her eyeliner, and reapplied her mascara. Depression lurked at the back of her consciousness. She could feel it, tangible and thick as quicksand.

"A damn sorry state of affairs," she whispered into the warm morning air. "What am I supposed to do?"

The question hung in her mind as she returned to the kitchen, packed lunch and high heels in a tote bag, and sat down to put on sneakers. The answer began as a tingle in her scalp. She did not feel the skin open and begin to tear. She did not feel it rip along the back of her head. All that happened was that a strange heaviness caught her attention.

Thinking her French braid had come undone, she reached back, only to feel something squish under her fingers. Her sagging scalp pressed down on her ears, and its full weight lay against her neck. The flesh underneath was soft and wet. The slime covered her hand and dripped onto her black-and-white designer dress.

Mariposa screamed only once before her jaw locked. Her body went on autopilot, jerking out of the chair, and whirling across the beige tiled floor to the shining stainless steel refrigerator in the corner. The world became dark and silent. Skin peeled off her body in long strips.

Her flesh turned dark gold and hardened. Gossamer cords spun from her skin and harnessed themselves to the freezer's metal handle. Mariposa now hung face down, at a forty-five degree angle from the door. Her French braid and designer dress lay in a messy heap on the floor.

What the hell's going on? Did I fall? Am I unconscious? I can't feel a thing! I can't see! I can't move! Oh, God... Am I blind? Paralyzed?

She thought of her body moving efficiently at her command, teaching, managing, achieving. She thought of never being able to move at all and panicked—but since she couldn't sob, scream, shake or vomit, she had no way to express it except through her thoughts. So, she thought a scream and followed it with another and another as her emotions roller-coastered from confusion to terror and back again. Then a sobering thought struck. *Maybe I'm dead.*

She considered that. No more grocery shopping, holiday planning or bills to pay. No more cooking, no more headaches, no more skin to pamper or fat cells to shrink. She allowed herself a mental chuckle. *Well, at least my sense of humor's intact. Dead, alive, blind or paralyzed, it'll come in handy, that's for sure.*

Something shifted. The shadow was on the move again. Its dark wave crested, steady and strong. She'd been trying to push it away since her hysterectomy three years ago. Her body protested with hot flashes, mood swings and heart palpitations, while her mind stubbornly denied her anger and fear. This time her body was not there for her to push around, and her mind was in no condition to deny anything. She felt the anger and the fear, but not the impulse to fight them. This time, she allowed the shadow to claim her.

Not used to stillness but having no other option, she let go. Memories and images of her life began to drift by, reminding her of fossils from the Pleistocene epoch—the kind you buy in souvenir shops in seaside tourist areas like Newport, Nantucket and Martha's Vineyard. Each detail embedded in the past, perfectly preserved in time.

Mariposa watched her seven-year-old self dig a hole in the backyard with the firm intention of reaching China before *The Muppet Show* came on. Her toy shovel never hit the feet of the people who walked upside down on the other side of the earth, but it did strike an arrowhead. Her chubby fingers pulled it out of the ground, and she wondered in amazement—Who had lived in her yard a long time ago? What kind of houses did they have? Did their little girls have dolls? She stood transfixed, wondering what else she'd find if she kept digging. So, she dug and dug until Mom called her in for supper.

She saw herself spread three arrowheads and two pieces of broken pottery on the table. But before she could ask Daddy her questions, Mom said, "Mariposa, get that dirt off my lace tablecloth and wash your hands. We are about to have supper!"

She and Daddy ate in silence. Mom prattled on about the church building fund and her charity work with the poor. Mariposa watched herself say a silent prayer. *Dear God, if you let me get big and dig in the ground to find out about stuff, I'll be a missionary. I'll go to Africa and save the souls of the savages.*

Mariposa watched as youthful idealism kept her passion strong through Mom's naysaying.

"You want to do what? Dig in the ground to find out how dead people lived? That makes no sense. It's wasted effort for a colored girl, Mariposa."

She saw her idealism crumble when she told her parents she planned to major in archaeology. Mom said, "Mariposa, Daddy and I are working hard to pay your tuition to make sure you'll have a stable future. Major in education, dear, that way you'll always have a job. You're the oldest. You need to set an example for your brother." Those words fell on fertile ground seeded with years of Mom's admonitions, unasked for advice, and family expectations.

She looked to Daddy for help. He cocked his head and shrugged.

Now, Mariposa watched herself major in education, graduate and tell her parents that she wanted to go to grad school, study archaeology, and travel to ancient sites around the world.

Mom looked up from her crocheting without missing a stitch and said, "What about Robert? I thought you two were getting married? He's a nice boy. Nice boys are hard to find, Mariposa. He may not be around when you come back from traipsing around the world. Marry Robert, dear. Build a safe and secure life for yourself, like Daddy and me. Work hard now. Your reward will come later."

She asked her father if he'd been rewarded for the hard work of his life. Daddy cocked his head and shrugged.

So, Mariposa watched herself rip up her application, marry Robert, and move to New England. Her dream was buried deep, and the idea of dreaming buried even deeper.

The memory shook her. A sudden, fierce desire rose from her core. She snatched the forgotten dream from the unexamined, dusty corners of her middle-aged mind. Waves of warm, golden light rippled over her body. The shadow began to recede. Sensation returned with a dry roasted taste in her mouth and a smoky smell in her nostrils.

Spasms tore through her body in waves. She shuddered as blood rushed through sleeping veins and arteries. Crawling sensations of pins and needles woke up her torso, arms, face, legs and feet. She wriggled past the discomfort, relieved beyond belief that she could move.

Something dry and hard blocked her. She pushed, pulled and twisted. It snapped, cracked and split. Mariposa flopped wet, weak and naked onto the cold hard tile of her kitchen floor. She sucked in long, deep breaths of air, opened her eyes, and looked around. Her first thought was, *Oh, thank God, I can see!* Her next was, *Oh, shit! What a mess!*

The six o'clock news and the voices of her children flowed from the den. *Oh, God... Bob and the kids!* She crawled over the kitchen floor to the dining room, struggled to her feet, and padded shakily across the carpet, leaving a trail of soggy footprints in the wheat-colored pile. She grabbed an old raincoat from the hall closet, tried to restore order to her hair, and headed toward the sounds.

Mariposa wanted to tell her family about her bizarre experience, but the normality of the scene stopped her cold.

"Woof!" Fishbourne, their Labradoodle, lumbered up from his pillow and began licking slime off her legs.

Bob looked up. "Oh, hi, hon. New hairdo? What's for dinner?"

"Motherrr! Randall's pickin' on me!" Delia's face was scrunched up in teenage angst.

"Am not!" yelled Randall. "I'm starvin', Ma! Where ya been?"

The everydayness of the scene threw her further off balance. She dream-walked back to the kitchen to clean up the mess and fix dinner. But there was no mess. The appliances sparkled. The tiled floor was clean and shiny. Her dress was folded neatly over the bar stool at the kitchen island, her tote bag beside it. Confused and overwhelmed, she went back to her family and offered them three options for dinner. They could warm up leftovers, eat frozen dinners from the freezer, or go to Mickey D's on the boulevard. Three astonished mouths gaped at her, while a bushy tail wagged with enthusiasm.

"I am going to take a long, hot bath!" Mariposa spun on her heel, locked the bathroom door, and turned on the faucets full force.

She had no idea what had happened or how her whole day could go missing, but she was sure of one thing. She had recovered an important piece of herself: a direction, a dream and a possibility not attached to job or family. It was hers and hers alone. She felt a rush of euphoria, a natural high, the biggest and baddest ever, as good as sex and better than chocolate. She hugged it to her heart and savored its sweetness.

The high didn't last, of course. It couldn't. After the bliss of rebirth wore off, uncertainty sank in. Was it real? Or had it been some sort of hallucination? Later that night, leaving out the weird happening in the kitchen, Mariposa told Bob about her dream of studying archaeology.

"Mariposa"—Bob looked at her over his horn-rimmed lawyer glasses—"why do you want to change careers? You're a teacher with job security." He paused. "We're not getting any younger, you know. We need to maximize our earning potential for retirement. Be sensible, Mariposa. We have to set an example for the kids. Our reward will come later."

Bob's words stunned Mariposa into silence. She had expected some measure of understanding and support. She was not prepared for an echo of her mother's words from long ago.

Over the next few weeks, Mariposa cooked, cleaned, carpooled and functioned as usual, but her strange experience refused to be ignored. She felt like a castaway with no bearings, with no landmarks or safe harbor on which to set her sights. Unable to move forward and unwilling to go back, she found herself stuck in a sad lateral drift, dog paddling to stay afloat.

She was torn. She could hardly perform a midlife disappearing act that left behind the wreckage of four hearts, three human and one canine. There had to be a way to move forward. She would find it. She had to! She couldn't talk to her husband, so after dinner one Saturday night, she sat on the porch and confided in the dog.

"Fishbourne, I have to do something, but I don't know what, and I need to talk to someone, but I don't know who."

"Woof," replied Fishbourne, lifting his ear for her to scratch with her long, red nails.

"What good is having a mystical experience if you can't figure out what you're supposed to do with it?"

Fishbourne nuzzled her cheek with his cold black nose, and they sat together on the front porch steps until the sun set.

Sunday dawned bright and warm. Mariposa fixed breakfast, served it in silence, and on impulse got dressed for church. She headed for Metropolitan AME Zion, a safe harbor for her storm-tossed soul. *I'm going to sing and pray these blues away today!* And indeed, Mariposa sang and prayed... but the blues stayed.

Weary, she headed home. Two blocks from the church, she passed a small brick duplex sandwiched between Brown's Furniture Warehouse and Mac's Liquor Store. A large wooden sign in the front yard read:

Lonely? Depressed? Scared?
Ask Miss Millie
Spiritual Adviser
Soul Food is our Signature Dish
Donations and Barter Accepted
All are Welcome!

She braked, backed up and parked in front of the duplex. "I must be crazy," she muttered. She stepped out of the car and walked to the front door. *If anyone sees me here, they'll know I'm one sandwich short of a picnic!*

She rang the bell. *Oh, God, I can't do this!* But before she could turn to leave, the front door opened and a tall, thin, ebony-skinned woman smiled at her. A starched white collar above a dark blue dress set off a halo of unpressed hair framing a kind face. An air of serenity softened the wrinkles around the woman's brown eyes and full mouth.

"Miss Millie?"

"Yes, child. Come in, sit down. I'll get you some lunch."

"Oh, I'm not hungry. I'm not even sure I should be here," said Mariposa.

"Nonsense," replied Miss Millie. "If you weren't supposed to be here, you wouldn't be. And we can't nurture the mind until we feed the body. Come in and rest yourself."

Miss Millie ushered Mariposa to a seat at the dining room table and fixed her a plate from the buffet. There was fried chicken, sweet potatoes, collard greens, buttermilk biscuits, peach cobbler and a tall glass of sweet tea. She sat across from Mariposa and said, "Now, how can I help you?"

Realizing she was hungry, Mariposa sipped her tea, then she cried and talked between mouthfuls of food until her story lay in heavy paragraphs and run-on sentences on Miss Millie's table.

"Sounds like a healing to me." Miss Millie's eyes were soft pools of compassion. "Sometimes, our shadow teaches us what the light cannot. Real or not doesn't matter. Was it an out-of-body experience? An alternate reality? A quantum entanglement? Everything is energy. Much of it remains a mystery." She beamed. "The important thing is, you were healed."

"I don't feel healed," Mariposa moaned. "I feel awful! I want my family, I want my life, and I want to stop this pain!"

"Of course you do! Healing is a messy, untidy business, but it's a gift. Time will teach you how to use it."

"How long will it take?" Mariposa groaned. "What do I have to do?"

Miss Millie leaned toward Mariposa. Her voice was gentle. "How long it will take and what you will need to do are the last issues to grapple with, dear. First, you must ask yourself two questions: 'What am I afraid of?' and 'Why am I afraid?' When you find answers to those questions, you will also find answers to 'How long will it take?' and 'What will I have to do?' Those are important questions. Listen for the answers. They are all around and within you. Be brave, diligent and patient. Trust your process."

Miss Millie's words—fresh, vital and wise—gave Mariposa the anchor she needed. She watched the sunlight kiss the windows, embrace the room, and gently encourage the leftover morning shadows to surrender their territory. She scooped up the last bite of peach cobbler and reached into her purse to make a donation. Miss Millie asked her to donate it to the local food bank instead. A grateful Mariposa thanked Miss Millie and went home.

On the way, she digested Miss Millie's soul food and wisdom. She accepted the challenge of her new beginning as the last remains of her shadow surrendered their hold on her heart.

"Bob?" He was reading a batch of papers. Lawyer stuff, she supposed.

"Hmm?"

"Can we talk?"

"Sure. Let me put this brief away. It can wait. What's up?"

"Well, I haven't had the chance to really respond to what we talked about last week."

"What do you mean, hon?"

"Remember the talk we had about me going back to school?"

"School?"

"Yes, to study archaeology."

Bob's left eyebrow twitched. "I thought we'd settled that."

"No-o-o. You stated your opinion. I didn't respond because I was surprised by your reaction." Mariposa felt her heart beat faster.

Bob stared straight at her. "My reaction surprised you." It was a statement, not a question.

"Yes, I thought you'd be more supportive."

"Supportive? Mariposa, we're talking about job security, family stability and college expenses for two children. We're talking about preparing for retirement. If I'm not mistaken, we agreed on all of it. Did I miss something?"

Mariposa heard Bob's impatience. Her heart sank. Despite her love for him and, she was sure, his love for her, they had their problems. When she wanted something for herself that did not have Bob or their family at its core, she felt selfish and guilty, and she usually gave in. *Not this time,* a little voice said. *Not this time.*

"No, you haven't missed anything, Bob. What makes you think going back to school will change our plans for the kids' college tuition and our retirement?"

"You don't know it won't." Another statement.

Mariposa spoke slowly and clearly to get her thoughts across. She wanted desperately to be logical because when she wasn't, Bob made her feel intellectually inferior.

"Well, I haven't explored all the options yet, but if it's possible, I want your support. I need to do this."

"No point in talking about it until you have facts. I can't commit support until I have details. Right now, it's too vague."

"I'm asking you to support me," Mariposa blurted out. "And I'm sitting right here in front of you. What's vague about that?" Her neck flushed and grew hot.

"See? You're getting all worked up. Of course, I support you. It's the situation I'm not sure of. Gather the facts, look at your options, and let's talk again." His let's-humor-her smile washed across his face. "You know I only want what's best for us. Anything else?"

The heat from Mariposa's neck spread up through the skin of her face and head. Her scalp prickled. "No. I guess not."

Feeling rattled as usual when she tried to talk to Bob about her needs and desires, Mariposa went for a walk to calm her nerves.

Why can't Bob understand? I don't neglect our family. Why is it so hard for me to get what I want? Why is Bob so hard-nosed and immovable about this? Why?

Talking to Fishbourne was a comfort, but now she needed a human being. She called the one who knew her best.

"Kevin?"

"Hey, Sis, what's up? You sound funny. Everything okay?"

"Bob and I had a fight..." Over the next few minutes, she filled him in on the details. "Talking to him about what I want is like talking to a brick wall," she sighed. "Or like talking to Mom. I never win. I wish I knew why."

"I know why."

"You do?"

"Yup."

Into the silence that followed, Mariposa asked, “Well?”

“Well what? Did you want me to tell you?”

“Yes, of course.”

“It’s not ‘of course’ to me, Sis. If you don’t ask, ain’t none of my business.”

“Kevin, I’m asking!”

“It’s simple. Folks like Mom and Bob like predictability—a place for everything and a place for everyone. Change upsets predictability.”

“Are you like that, Kev?”

“Damn right. That’s why I’m not married. Haven’t met a woman I could predict for longer than a minute, and them ain’t good odds for the long term. I’d rather have a dog.”

“Kevin, what an awful thing to say!”

“Maybe, but it’s the truth, and you know I’d never lie to you. Problem is, you want change. You bumped up against Mom growing up, and now you’re bumping up against Bob. And you’re afraid that if you put your foot down to get what you want, he will start resenting you like you resented Mom.”

Mariposa opened her mouth to protest, but no words came out.

“And before you go all defensive, remember, Mom pushed people to do what she wanted. You need to push for yourself. That’s the difference. Seems to me you got a clear path, Sis. Either do it or don’t. You got consequences both ways, and you may not like either set, but you’ve spent your whole life doing what others want. Might be time to do you.”

“Kevin, you’d make a great shrink.”

“Nuh-uh. I can talk to you about stuff ’cause we’re kin; couldn’t, wouldn’t do it with strangers. Too much hassle.”

“Love you, Kev.”

“Love you too, Sis. Look, um, I gotta go. This is too mushy for me.”

That's so Kevin, Mariposa thought, smiling to herself at her brother's reluctance to show emotion. "Okay, Kev. Bye."

Mariposa's spine stiffened with resolve. The next few days were busy. She made calls to the state university and several area colleges. *It's got to be in-state or there's no way I can manage this,* she decided. *Can't even think about talking to Bob yet. One thing at a time, Mariposa. One thing at a time...*

A few weeks later, she was ready. It was a lazy Saturday night. The kids were out, and Bob and she were sitting in the den. The evening news was over. Mariposa would typically pick out a book to read while Bob clicked around until he found a sporting event to watch, usually golf or basketball.

"Bob?"

"Uh-huh?"

She laid out her plan step by step. The state university was affordable. The inheritance her parents left her would cover the cost. Two classes a semester, two nights a week at most. Also, there was summer school, which would speed things up. With luck, she could be done in two years. Their savings would not be touched. The retirement funds would not be touched. The kids' college funds would not be touched. She would not have to leave her job, so her financial contribution to the household would remain the same.

Believing she had addressed every possible objection, challenge and cross-examination Bob could make, she smiled. "What do you think?"

"What about your energy? For the past three years, you've been complaining about being tired, and that's with your normal activities. Now you're talking about adding something. How will this affect your energy?"

She hadn't seen that one coming at all. "I don't think it'll be a problem. After all, it's something I've always wanted to do, something I've always loved."

"I thought you loved your family."

"Of course I do! This is different!"

"Oh? How is it different? We make you tired, and this won't, and there's no difference?"

Mariposa's heart sank. "Bob, please try to understand. I love you. I love the kids. But this is something I want to do for me."

"Sounds selfish, if you ask me."

"But why? I'm not taking anything away from us. I'm not giving up my responsibilities."

"Because, Mariposa, everything I do relates to my job or my family. I don't want anything else. Why do you need more? Isn't your job and our family enough? You need to think a bit more about this."

Mariposa's anger flared in her gut. She tried to stuff it, but it would not stay stuffed. She felt an intense desire to rip the flesh off her husband's face. The rage burned brighter. She blocked it, but it would not stay blocked. When it reached her heart, it turned to tears. She stifled them, but they would not stay stifled. When the tears passed her throat, they turned into a silent scream of anguish. She was grateful for the silence. When they reached her mouth, she had to choke back the urge to curse. When they passed her eyes, they exploded into a headache so intense she had to grip the arms of her chair.

"I can't believe you are being so unreasonable with me," she finally got out.

"Unreasonable? I simply asked you to think about the impact of your actions on our family. That doesn't sound unreasonable to me."

"That's not what I meant."

"Then you'd better start saying what you mean because I can only respond to what I hear. Do we need to talk about this anymore tonight?"

It was over. He'd done it again. "No, no, I guess not."

Bob turned back to his golf match. Mariposa left the den, went into the bathroom, and sat on the toilet for a good cry.

This time, they were not tears of sadness. They were tears of frustration. God! How could two people who loved each other get into such a stinking, unfair mess!

Sometimes she pined for the wild abandon of their early days. She had opened herself completely to him. She'd been spontaneous and free, a feeling she had not experienced growing up in her mother's constrained and proper home. However, over their years together, she had come to understand that what Bob had loved in her as his girlfriend was not something he wanted to see in his wife. He wanted predictability, like Kevin had said. She had met that need with Bob as she had with her mother, and so she'd been denying her own wants and needs.

No more! As she sat and seethed, something shifted, transforming her rage and frustration into a deep sense of calm. Her mind, heart and gut lined up behind her will.

She strode back to the den. This time, her voice was firm, confident and direct.

"You know Bob, I spend too much time trying to convince you to see things from my point of view. If I want something for myself, you see it as desertion. You pull out your brand of lawyer logic and hammer me into emotional pulp. I know you don't do it to be mean, but that's how it comes across. I let your needs and the kids' needs dictate how I spend my life, and it's eating me alive. This changes now!"

"Whoa, wait a minute, tiger! This is about you going back to school isn't it? I thought we settled this. I've told you how I feel."

"Have you listened to anything I've said?"

"Of course I listened. I can tell you word for word what you said."

"Good. Then keep your ears open because now I'm going to tell you what I'm going to do."

Bob's eyes widened.

"I put my dream off to please my mother. I put it off to marry you. I put it off to raise the kids." She paused. "The application for grad school is on my desk. Tomorrow morning, I'm going to fill it out and send it in. I hope you'll support my decision, but I don't need your support to do this. I need my own, and it's about damn time I realized it!"

Bob's mouth gaped open, then closed. He pursed his lips and stared at Mariposa as though she'd suddenly turned green and grown horns. "Don't you think—?"

"No! I don't think, Bob, I know! I know exactly what I'm doing."

Bob cocked his head and shrugged.

That's it? No drama? She'd steeled herself to push through Bob's cast-iron resistance to her declaration of independence. Instead, she'd gotten a resigned head tilt and shrug—exactly like her father's.

Her brother's words floated through her mind. "Might be time to do you."

Indeed, she thought. *Indeed. At last, it's time to do me. It's time for me to spread my wings and fly.*

A Stitch in Time

Claudette is a figment of my imagination, but Rebecca Primus was a real person who lived in the 1800s. Threads of history, adversity and resilience weave their stories together, even though they take place centuries apart.

Claudette Boyd reached out a hand to flush the toilet as a familiar voice floated over the stall door. It was Kerry.

"When is Claudette gonna stop moaning about her problems? Every day, the same thing. I swear, Ginger, I don't know how long I can be a guest at her pity party."

Claudette's hand froze in midair.

"Yeah." Ginger's voice joined the assault on Claudette's ears. "Maybe we should nominate her for this month's PMS poster girl!"

"Good idea," said Kerry, "except for the fact her time of the month lasts all year round."

Their laughter shook Claudette to the core with a 9.9 on her emotional Richter scale. The aftershocks rattled then gradually subsided, but they left her trembling, agitated and angry. She waited for the click of the restroom door to assure herself that she was alone. Only then did she flush the toilet, exit the stall, and wash her hands. The sound of running water rinsed away her dark thoughts, leaving sadness in their wake as she returned to her desk.

Oh, man! Am I really that bad? she thought. *Pity party? I know I gripe and grumble, but I'm no different from anyone else—am I? Don't we all complain? Let me take stock. Yes, I hate my job. Processing insurance applications is boring. I hate working in this environment. It's all small, tacky cubicles, brown partitions, and barf-beige walls.*

A slow sigh escaped her full lips. *I'm Black, female, close to forty and single. I hate this city 'cause there's nothing to do and there are no good men around. They're too tall, too short, too cheap, too loud, too quiet, too macho, too country or too slick. I hate the way I look. My hips are too big, my boobs are too small, and my legs are too thin. I'm not crazy about my family either. My brothers are loud, my sisters are bitchy, Dad's a couch potato, and Mom has more shoulds and oughts than the law allows. Shit! I really am the PMS poster girl!*

With that realization, Claudette sank into a deep blue funk.

After work, she raced home to her apartment and wrapped its warm comfort around her wounded soul. She nuked a halfway healthy microwave dinner of chicken, turnips and broccoli, then topped it off with a glass of her favorite red wine.

Feeling somewhat better after dinner, she poured another glass of Merlot and moved from her green-and-white kitchen to her lavender-and-white bedroom to change into her pajamas. She hopped on the bed, plumped up four lace-trimmed satin pillows, tucked them behind and alongside her, and reached for the pile of fabric on the far side of the bed.

Despite her complaints and the lists of things she hated, Claudette had a deep and abiding passion for fabrics and textiles. In her spare time, she designed pillow covers, window treatments and quilts, which she sold at craft fairs and online through her website stitch-in-time.com. A trip to the fabric store was her idea of Heaven. The bolts of potential, bright colors of creation and a multitude of possibilities made the back of her neck tingle, and in short order, those possibilities found their way into her sales inventory and decorations for her home. Once in a while, she dreamed of having her own brick-and-mortar store, but fear of failure and a sense of inadequacy kept her tied to her cubicle at work where—as Kerry and Ginger had cruelly but truthfully pointed out—she complained long, loud and often about her life.

On her lap lay a free-form quilt made of leftover scraps from other projects. Pinned to the base fabric was a motif of multicolored flowers, leaves, vines and tree branches spreading in wild abandon over the off-white background. Claudette reached for the remote and clicked on the TV sitting at eye level in the oak entertainment center. A bit of background noise would provide a soothing environment to help her focus.

She surfed through the channels. Boring reality shows, celebrity chefs cooking, fake doctors saving fake lives, cops chasing crooks, lame family sitcoms, men running on football fields and shooting hoops in crowded gyms, muscled bodies crunching, soap operas dishing, news reporters reporting, political pundits punditing, a Black woman smiling... *Wait! What's this?* Claudette put the remote down. It was the local public broadcasting channel, and the narrator was talking about the nineteenth century and the lives of free Blacks.

History had never been one of Claudette's favorite subjects. It ranked right up there on her "prefer to avoid" list with math and science. However, relaxed by her wine and pleased that she'd found a distraction with some relevance to her existence, Claudette picked up her needle and thread from the nightstand and began sewing her garden fantasy design to the base fabric with small, neat stitches.

The camera zoomed out to a wide shot. The smiling woman wore a belled taffeta dress with wide sleeves. The bodice and skirt were trimmed with black velvet ribbons, with an intricate, beige lace collar at the high, round neckline. Her long, braided hair, parted in the middle, wrapped itself around her head coronet style. Walnut-brown skin made a pleasant contrast to the black and burgundy of the dress. The narrator stopped narrating and as the background music faded, the smiling woman spoke.

"My name is Rebecca Primus."

She walked to a chair placed center stage and sat down. Her sharp eyes looked out at her television audience.

"I am a teacher. And in 1867, I founded the first school for Africans in Royal Oak, Maryland. This is my story."

"Iszat so?" muttered Claudette as she began to stitch around the petals of a large red flower. Talking back to the television was high on her list of solitary pleasures; a one-way conversation with no possibility of rebuttal, made for therapeutic venting.

Next to Rebecca's chair stood a small, round table bearing a flowered porcelain teapot with a companion cup and saucer. As she spoke, Rebecca poured herself a cup of tea.

"I was born in 1836 in Hartford, Connecticut, the first of four children. Henrietta came next, then Nelson and finally Isabel, and since she was the baby, we all spoiled her, especially Father."

A stab of envy shot through Claudette, making the next few stitches ragged.

"I'm glad some-damn-body got spoiled. I sure never did." Claudette's eyes radiated irritation and residual childhood pain. "You try being the middle child in a family of five. Huh! I felt like wilted lettuce in a day-old ham and cheese sandwich!"

Rebecca lifted the cup and saucer from the table and placed it on her lap.

"Father was an officer in the Talcott Street Congregational Church, a founding member of the Hartford chapter of the Prince Hall Masons, and well thought of by the White citizenry.

He was always able to find work as a servant or a porter. Mother gardened, sewed, kept chickens in the backyard, and had her own business training domestic workers. Together, they saved every penny they could, and in 1849, when I was thirteen, Father bought a house on Wadsworth Street in the White neighborhood—an astonishing achievement for a colored man at that time."

Claudette picked up a newly threaded needle, savagely bit off the thread with her teeth, deftly knotted the end with one hand, and began working on a curling green vine. "Yeah, well..." she began. "White neighborhoods aren't all they're cracked up to be, honey. I know. I grew up as the only and the lonely, the grain of pepper in the salt, the raisin in the milk, the... well, you get the picture. Shoot, girlfriend, I spent half my life trying to find a way to fit in. The White kids didn't play with me cause I was Black, and the Black kids wouldn't play with me cause they said I wasn't Black enough! Talk about being out of place in every space!"

Claudette's mood darkened. She sucked her teeth and glowered at Rebecca, who paused, took a sip of tea while ignoring Claudette, and continued her story.

"I went to the North African School at the Talcott Street Congregational Church. Rev. J. W. C. Pennington and his wife encouraged my natural bent for learning, and from them, I developed a desire to take my knowledge and use it for racial uplift. It was a dream that burned deep in my heart. I wanted my people to have full citizenship. I knew we would accomplish this when more of us could read and write. So, I determined to become a teacher."

Claudette took a sip of wine and shifted her body to ease the pins and needles in her legs.

"So, you had a dream! Well, la de da! Move over, Dr. King, and make way for Miss Thang and her dream. Humph! Bet you ended up cleaning pots in Miss Ann's kitchen!"

Rebecca placed the cup on the saucer in her left hand.

"I prayed and worked hard, and at long last, my dream came true."

For the second time that day, Claudette's hand froze in midair. "It came true?" she asked. "Well, how, pray tell, did you manage that, missy? Best you put that teacup down and talk to me!"

As though in response, Rebecca placed the cup and saucer in the center of the little table.

"The great Civil War was almost over. The United States Congress was funding the Freedmen's Bureau to care for the needs of newly freed slaves. The White citizens of Hartford formed a chapter of the Freedmen's Aid Society for the purpose of sending teachers south to help freed slaves learn to read and write. There were many desirous of such an appointment, and the society interviewed us all several times before they made their selection. I give thanks to this day that I was one of five offered the position. And in November 1865, I boarded the train to Baltimore and took a carriage to Royal Oak, Maryland, to begin the greatest adventure of my life."

"Whoa! You go, girl! Spread your nappy little wings and fly!" Now genuinely interested in Rebecca's story, Claudette's head shook from side to side as she stitched. "Shoot, I can't even get my wings to flap."

Rebecca stood and smoothed the folds of her skirt. They rustled in harmony with the music of her voice. "I met with the Royal Oak Association for the Moral and Educational Improvement of Colored People, and by December 1865, I taught at a school in the church. I began with ten children in the day class and twenty-six adults at night. The number of eager scholars soon increased to seventy-five. Oh, what thrilling, rewarding work it was, and how wonderful to see the scales of ignorance fall away from the eyes of young and old alike! Even so, I missed life in Hartford, and I especially missed my good friend Addie Brown."

Claudette grimaced. "If she was anything like Kerry and Ginger, you didn't miss anything, sister-girl. If those two heifers were really my friends, they'd get in my face and tell me what they're thinking instead of gossiping behind my back."

Rebecca's smile broadened. "We wrote each other constantly during those years. I could be quite free with Addie, and my letters to her were full of my adventures. In my letters to Father and Mother, I was more careful and reassuring. I did not want them to worry about me. However, all reassurances aside, there were dangers. There was much sickness among the people—cholera, smallpox, typhoid and measles, to name a few—and the Ku Klux Klan night raids, rallies and cross burnings were quite terrifying."

"Yeah, and back then, you didn't have anything in your carpet bag to kill the germs or the bigots!" Claudette grinned, pleased at her little joke. "Sounds pretty gruesome to me. So, how did you keep your stuff together, Becky Baby?"

Rebecca stood, walked to the back of the brown Shaker-style chair, and placed two slender hands atop the rail. Her eyes stared straight into Claudette's.

"Faith in God and a firm belief in my mission gave me the strength to persevere."

"Oh, I see. On top of everything, you a churchified sister!" Claudette rolled her eyes and shook her head, but kept listening.

"All this new experience was quite exhilarating! I taught day and evening classes, and Sunday school. I was a soldier in the front line of the greatest battle this country would ever face. So, I determined to build my own school to accommodate everyone who wanted to attend classes. The Talcott Street Church in Hartford raised two hundred dollars. The colored community in Royal Oak held student exhibitions and church fairs. The Southern Rights men donated lumber, a sign that their hearts were beginning to soften. The New York Freedmen's Aid Society purchased the land. And in September 1867, the great day dawned and the Primus Institute opened. There were speeches, recitals and ice cream. What a glorious day! Mother and Father were so proud of me. Truth be told, it was one of the most wonderful days of my life."

The only sound coming from Claudette now was the soft swish of thread through fabric.

"Things continued in that vein for another two years. Then disaster struck."

Claudette looked up. "Uh-huh... No surprise. I knew it was too good to be true. Always happens. Here comes some stuff!"

Rebecca returned to the front of the chair, sat, folded her hands in her lap and looked up. "Reconstruction ended and the Freedmen's Bureau was dissolved by Congress. Imagine. The one bright light to help my people improve themselves after years of enslavement and injustice... struck down. It was a sad day for many, and a time of great disillusionment for me. With the Freedmen's Bureau gone, the Hartford chapter disbanded and called its teachers home."

Claudette put her needle down. "Ha! Your dream got deferred after all!" Her satisfaction at being proven right was tinged with compassion, a feeling Claudette did not have in large supply, for herself or anyone else.

A sad look replaced the broad smile on Rebecca's face. "So much work left undone. There were three thousand teachers in the South. When we were called home, all efforts to stem the tide of illiteracy among colored people were simply washed away. I couldn't believe my eyes when the letter came. In that instant, all my hopes and dreams were brutally crushed. I watched my efforts and those of so many others crumble into dust in no more time than it took to swat a fly. The weight of it sent me to my knees. I felt my faith in God slipping. I knew if I lost it, I might never get up again.

"I prayed and clung desperately to my faith. Finally, with great difficulty, I accepted the inevitable, gave my burden over to the Lord, and rose from my knees to fall into an exhausted sleep. In the morning, I closed my school and boarded the train for home. Once settled back into family and church, I sought a teaching position in Hartford, but Connecticut had done away with separate schools, and the new integrated schools hired only White teachers. My teaching career was over."

Claudette tsk'd and humph'd as she began work on one of the stout tree branches. She felt a kinship with Rebecca, validated by her interpretation of mutual misfortune. "I knew the deck would get stacked against you, somehow, someway. It always does. Can't catch a break, so why bother to try. This world can't wait to find ways to hold a Black woman down and push her back. Guess you found that out too!"

But Rebecca smiled.

"In order to make a useful living, I became a seamstress working with Mother."

"Well, damn, girl! It's not Miss Ann's kitchen, but it's close. Imagine that. A hundred and twenty-something years apart and we're both stitching. You to make a living, and me to keep from going postal." Claudette's laughter ricocheted off the bedroom walls.

Rebecca went on. "I resolved to be the best seamstress I could be. It was not easy. Letting dreams go is hard work. In my time, women did not have many choices, so I learned to be content with my life."

Suddenly, Claudette felt a "fabric store tingle" at the back of her neck as an idea formed. "Hmm, if you and your mom could run a business a century ago, I ought to be able to run one now. As bad as things are, I can vote, own property, and get credit in my own name. That's way more choice than you had, Rebecca. Way more."

As Claudette finished the last stitch in the tree branch, she made a decision. "Kerry and Ginger are right. I need to change."

Rebecca, meanwhile, rose from the chair and took a step forward.

"Death comes for us all. It came for me in 1932. I was ninety-six. You may think from what I've told you that I was not happy with my life. Not so. Even though my dream died too quickly, it did live. I was a teacher. I did help my people. I made a difference. This is what sustained me through my hard times. I believe we must face our difficulties bravely and work diligently to make our dreams real. We may experience success or failure, but whatever our experience, we must try. That is, I think, what makes us truly human."

Music swelled. Rebecca smiled. Credits rolled.

Claudette yawned and stretched. "Well, maybe I *will* do something about my business." She stuck the needle into the spool of thread and placed it on the nightstand. Her voice became a whisper, "Yeah, like Sam Cooke said, 'a change gonna come.'"

She folded the quilt, put it to one side and slid under the covers. "First thing tomorrow, I'll start working up a business plan. Yes, first thing tomorrow. For now, I'll... just... sleep on it."

Claudette's eyes closed, and soon she was fast asleep underneath her lavender-and-white comforter.

Rebecca Primus folded her hands in front of her skirt. Her soft gaze came to rest on Claudette's sleeping form.

"Good night, Claudette," said Rebecca as the screen slowly faded to black.

1-800-555-MARY

Learning to love oneself is the foundation of self-respect, self-acceptance and self-care. It requires self-awareness—and sometimes tough love.

I'd picked up my cell phone to call Charlaine when I looked out the window—and there it was. Smiling pink lips, pale blue eyes, and slim white hands folded in prayer. Above a golden halo were the words "Virgin Mary Speaks to America Today." Underneath the hands was a telephone number with the instruction "Call 1-800-555-MARY." I stopped dead in my tracks and laughed before I got mad. I spent at least ten minutes with my hands on my hips and my eyes all squinty, trying to figure out what that billboard was doing in my neighborhood. I was used to the ones that sold Kool cigarettes, Boone's Farm wine, and Ford Mustangs, and I wondered how much Madison Avenue planned to charge for salvation.

She looked like the models on those other billboards. Size 10, thin, pretty in a washed-out, Eurocentric kind of way. I snorted. What a loony tunes world! The Black Madonna is front and center in many French churches, and here's a White Madonna on top of the Nation of Islam's mattress factory. Go figure!

Maybe I wouldn't have been so irreverent if she looked more like the women I knew, but that blonde hair and those blue eyes were a bit much to swallow in a neighborhood where most folks ranged from café au lait brown to pitch purple-black with soft dark eyes and lots of too, too solid flesh.

"Too, too solid flesh." That's Shakespeare. It's from *Hamlet*. I'd always liked it because I'd been trying to melt my too, too solid flesh for too, too, too many years.

I was 250 pounds and counting when Oprah went through her weight thing. She got into those size 10 jeans and strutted on stage, and I gave it up for her. "You go, girl!" I screamed. "You go for all of us!"

Then she had to drop the size 10 when she ballooned back into 16s and 18s. I was crushed. Finally, she hired a personal chef and a trainer and found a happy medium.

I was glad for her, but I couldn't afford a personal chef or a trainer, so instead I called 1-800-94-JENNY. I tried Nutrisystem, Weight Watchers and Overeaters Anonymous. I did the grapefruit plan, the protein plan, the Keto plan, and the low-fat plan. I sweated to the oldies, took pills and even paid a three-month visit to Mama Rue's fat farm in the Caribbean. For a New York minute, I even thought about having my stomach stapled. Dumped that idea, then gave up trying.

It was the breakdown that finally did me in. After that happened, I just sat around the apartment, watching TV and talking to Charlaine whenever I could get a word in edgewise around her advice about what I should be doing with my life. Charlaine is my best friend, you see. We used to talk on the phone during *Oprah*, swapping opinions about her diets, hair, clothes and guests.

Delores and Charlaine, two sister-friends passing the time. Because of our friendship, and only because of it, I listened and nodded and said things like, "Uh-huh," "I know you're right," and "Okay, I'll think about that." But my depression weighed more than I did, so I did nothing.

The last time we talked, I could tell she was all kinds of upset with me. "Dee," she said, "you have got to pull yourself together. I'm all outta advice. I don't know how else to help you." She sighed. "And you know I want to. We've been ride-or-die friends since the third grade, and if you can't dig yourself out of this hole, you leave me no choice but to figure out how to hold an intervention on your behind!"

The breakdown? Oh, yeah, that. Well, it had been coming on for a while. I could feel it sneaking up my spine, looking for attention, but I got really good at pushing that shadow back into its hole. Food, sex and shopping worked until they didn't, and I'd pretty much reached the end of my rope when I walked into the cafeteria at work that day. The lights were too bright, the noise was too loud, and I swore I could feel bugs crawling up my legs. I stood stock-still, dropped my tray, and commenced to cuss, shake and howl something awful.

Next thing you know, I'm in a straitjacket at the local loony bin, popping Valium like it's aspirin. The shrink they sent me to didn't have a clue, so as soon as I stopped raving, they gave me a prescription for antidepressants and let me go.

They didn't know what was wrong. But I did. I felt unloved. Sure, Charlaine and my family loved me, but theirs was the safe love that families and friends are supposed to have for one another. I was missing the bone-deep, totally accepting love, the kind that wraps around your life and bursts your heart. And it wasn't about men. Many had declared their love for my soft eyes, my ample curves, my southern fried chicken, and my sweet potato pie. I felt their arms and heard their words, but I never believed they were really meant for me.

Anyway, my depression and I holed up in my apartment. When I needed to talk, I called Charlaine. When I needed food, I called Stop and Shop.

My job had given me a six-week medical leave to get myself together and go back to work. With three weeks to go, I was nowhere near ready and really bummed out. Giving up my job as a systems analyst and not working at all was scary. The thought of going back to work and facing everybody made my insides quake, but I knew I couldn't make it on welfare. Too humiliating. I felt like Mount St. Helens before her big bang.

The Mary billboard was just another irritant. And that irritant started to watch me. Her eyes followed me around my living room. They reproached me when I ate, pleaded soulfully with me when I watched TV, and got a hopeful glint in them when I talked to Charlaine. I could feel those eyes glued on me like white on rice. The feeling persisted even when I pulled down the shade.

So that's how it was when I woke up three weeks before my day of reckoning. I heaved myself out of bed and waddled past the window to pick up the remote control. I was going to watch the *Today* show and try to ignore Mary like I usually did, but that morning something pulled my eyes to the window and glued them square on the billboard.

My jaw dropped. Her eyes had changed color. Now they were brown—a soft, warm, sparkling brown. I shook my head and looked again. No mistake. *Strange*, I thought. *Why would they come back and just change the color of her eyes?*

The next day, her blonde hair turned dark brown and started to curl. After that, her skin darkened, her nose broadened, her lips widened, her hair kinked up, and she started gaining weight. I sat by the window night after night, trying to catch the midnight painter, but despite NoDoz and extra coffee, I never saw a soul. Yet each morning, Mary looked more and more like a fat Black Madonna with a 'fro. But her mouth still wore that lush, glowing smile, and her eyes continued to haunt me.

Many times during those days, I felt an urge to pick up the phone and make the call. Many times my hand reached out and just as many times I snatched it back. I knew the billboard didn't make any rational sense, and I am basically a rational and intelligent person. Except for my breakdown, I tend to carefully plan my idiocies. I knew I wasn't hallucinating because I had flushed all the medications from the hospital down the toilet. Reality was bad enough without drugs. I was depressed and dysfunctional—not delusional.

Finally, when I couldn't stand it a minute longer, I pulled my hand out of a bag of double chocolate macadamia nut cookies, pushed the bottle of Diet Coke aside, heaved myself up from the couch, grabbed my phone, and punched in the numbers: 1-8-0-0-5-5-5-M-A-R-Y.

I heard it ring on the other end, and I started to sweat. It rang again, and I began to panic. It rang a third time, and I was about to hang up when someone answered. A voice warm enough to melt frozen butter in a nanosecond said, "Hello-o-o."

"Uh, hi. Uh, can I speak to Mary, please?"

"Oh, sure, honey. Is this Delores Gray?"

"Uh... uh... Yeah, this is me," I said as I peered around my apartment. "Listen, am I on *Candid Camera*?"

The voice chuckled. "No, sugar. This is for real. Hang on a minute, will you? She's just getting off the other line."

The other line? Why, I wondered, did this feel like a call to the Psychic Friends Network? I looked around for Dionne Warwick.

"Listen, dear, you *will* hang on. Won't you?"

Well, really, what did I have to lose? "Yeah, I'll wait," I managed to croak.

There was something disturbingly familiar about Mary's voice when she came on the line. In a way, it was like listening to the women in my family. The cadence, pitch, tone and accent were right on the mark, yet it was different somehow. I couldn't place it, and that unsettled me.

"Delores, what took you so long? I've been waiting and waiting to hear from you."

"You have?" My eyebrows shot up to meet my hairline.

"Yes. We've been trying to get through to you for weeks."

"Really?" I put my free hand on my hip, popped it out, and sucked on my teeth.

"Yes! We tried reaching you through your family and Charlaine. You weren't listening. You know, Delores, you're running out of time. We had to resort to something dramatic."

I rolled my eyes. "Uh-huh, and you thought a billboard of the Virgin Mary would be just the thing to get my attention?"

"Well, we send out the word as best we can, but it doesn't always get through the way we intend it. The veil between us is very thin, dear, but it can cloud up."

I sighed. What kind of scam was this woman running?

"The billboard designer and Father O'Leary didn't get the image right. We had to alter it to make our point. I hope it didn't upset you too much."

It didn't compute. Maybe I was having some kind of post-drug hallucination. Discomfort and confusion coalesced and turned into a nasty hunch. The hair on the back of my neck stood up. My head felt poufy like cotton candy. Suddenly, I knew why the voice was so familiar. It was woo-woo time.

"Your name's not really Mary, is it?" I whispered.

"No," she said softly.

"Who the hell are you?" I rasped.

"I think you know."

"Maybe, but I want to hear you say it."

"My name is Delores, and I love you."

The weight of those words knocked me off my feet and sat me down on the couch. I was talking to myself! I was talking to the part of me that had never given up; the part I ignored and shunted aside; the part that knew the truth about my inability to feel love; the part that recognized my feelings of insecurity, vulnerability and pain; the part that sent me off the deep end, hoping I'd find a way to climb back up.

"Delores?"

I sniffled. "Yes."

"Are you still listening?"

I gulped. "Yes."

"Can you love me back?"

"It's hard," I gasped. "I... I don't know how."

"Too hard to love yourself? Oh, dear, maybe I'm too late after all. Should I hang up?"

"No-o-o!" I screamed into the phone. "No-o-o! No-o-o!"

"Way to go, dear. I think you need a little more time to pull yourself together. How about two weeks?"

Two weeks later, I went back to work and rejoined the human race. I recycled the Diet Coke bottles, started drinking lemon water, and added fruits and vegetables to my Stop and Shop deliveries. I had a heart-to-heart with Charlaine and told her I needed to see a new shrink, someone with some common sense.

"I've been waiting for you to get to this point." She said. "Now here's what you do. You pick up your phone, and you call Frank Rutledge. He's a brother, and he's smart as hell. Aunt Delesta and Uncle Sanders are going to see him for marriage counseling. Oh, and did I mention he was cute?"

I took down his number, but it took me a few days to screw up my courage and make an appointment. My experience with shrinks is not a pretty picture. But when a good friend like Charlaine does the recommending, the least I can do is try.

The fact that Delesta and Sanders were trusting him to help them was comforting. Charlaine's relatives have been part of my family in the same way that mine are part of hers. Small towns and close-knit communities are like that. Sometimes, it truly does take a village.

Delores-Mother-Mary-Me was right. I'm working on loving myself as I am: big, Black and bodacious.

Charlaine was right about Dr. Rutledge. It's slow going, but I'm making progress. I've even started singing again. As a kid, I sang in the church choir, then choral groups in high school, and an a cappella group in college. I dropped the singing when I started working and forgot about it altogether when the "troubles" started.

Oh, and I'm still giving it up for Oprah. If she knew about my struggle, I know she'd give it up right back and scream, "You go, Delores! You go for all of us!"

Note: The original of this story first appeared in the 2020 edition of *The Connecticut Literary Anthology* and has been revised and expanded for this collection.

The Enlightenment of Franklin Rutledge

Being able to reflect honestly on our thinking and behavior is key to living with clarity, contentment and resilience. This is the story of how Franklin Rutledge came to that realization.

The silver Jaguar eased into a reserved parking space at Brookside Counseling Center. The driver's door opened. A pair of tasseled brown loafers emerged, followed by a pair of dark brown slacks topped by a brown-and-white, open-collar pinstriped shirt and a tweed jacket. The tall, handsome man lit a handcrafted pipe; ran a manicured hand through his soft, wavy brown curls; grabbed a briefcase from the back seat; and trotted his Harvard-educated body up the front steps.

His day as Dr. Franklin Rutledge, PhD, clinical psychologist, had begun. He was full of himself, and well he should have been. After all, he'd come a long way from his poverty-stricken childhood in Natchitoches, Louisiana. He'd worked hard, focused on his goals and not rested until he earned his doctorate. Even then, the rest was momentary.

In short order, he secured the right job, the right wife and the right house, along with carefully selected professional, social and community connections. He still had the right job, the right connections and the right house, but the right wife was gone.

Despite the divorce, Franklin remained on a mission to show tortured souls how to live happy, productive lives according to his formula. He took the elevator to the fourth floor, entered the hushed atmosphere of his waiting room, and nodded to the woman seated behind the counter.

"What do we have today, Ms. Burke?"

Leola Burke was Franklin's receptionist. She smiled at "her" doctor.

"You've got the Hobsons at ten, lunch with Councilman Burns at noon. At two o'clock, it's a family session with Harrison Parker, his parents and his husband. They've scheduled six sessions—sounds serious. Your last appointment is a four o'clock meeting at city hall to work on plans for the free clinic." She handed him a clipboard with the schedule.

"Thank you, Ms. Burke. Let me know when the Hobsons arrive."

Franklin had been reluctant to counsel couples since his divorce. He was uncertain about his ability to help others after failing to save his own marriage. He'd taken this session with the Hobsons as a way to dip his toe back into the couples counseling pool. He'd brushed up on the latest marriage theories, read the relevant research, and consulted several of his professional colleagues. He was ready.

After a few minutes, Leola peered through the door and announced, "They're here, Doctor."

Delesta Hobson was well dressed and carried her medium build and warm beige complexion confidently, but the look on her face was one of frustration.

Sanders Hobson was tall, thin and Black as the proverbial berry. His shoulders drooped and his head listed to the left, an indication, thought Franklin, of long-suffering resignation, as he moved from his desk to the easy chair and seated the Hobsons on the couch.

Once pleasantries were out of the way, he opened his notebook and asked Mrs. Hobson to start.

Delesta leaned forward, parted her full lips, and held nothing back.

"You want to know why we're here? It's simple. Little Miss Fix-It got no more Band-Aids in her medicine chest of love. For thirty-nine years, I've tweaked myself here, changed myself there, altered this behavior, and that way of speaking to make this marriage work. I've turned a deaf ear to this and a blind eye to that. I'm wrung out and drained dry. This is a last ditch effort. If counseling doesn't work, I'm filing for divorce. I've got a right to my peace of mind. I'm pissed as hell, and I'm not gonna take it anymore!"

Sanders, who had been listening quietly, now jumped in. "I'm plenty ticked off m'damn self. I don't like gettin' personal with strangers—I like my privacy. But since she's threatenin' to file for divorce, I don't have much choice. I know my wife is upset. I think it's a matter of ego and a loss of perspective. I think we can work this out by ourselves if she'd listen to me for a minute. I mean, I hold down a full-time job, come home dog-tired each night, eat dinner, and watch a little TV before bed. I deposit my check in the bank every two weeks. I don't screw around with money or other women. I don't drink or bad-mouth my wife in public. But I don't get much appreciation for my efforts."

Franklin may have been intellectually ready to help the Hobsons, but he was not prepared for his visceral reaction to their story. Replay the same scene with different voices and syntax, and you had Marceline and Franklin Rutledge. Franklin had protested bitterly when Marceline warned him she'd file for divorce unless he came to couples counseling. He'd also worried about the professional disgrace if his peers found out. In the end, he'd agreed, but counseling hadn't helped. Despite his intellectual rationalizations, the divorce left him raw and emotional.

"Maybe I've been too nice!" declared Sanders, sitting back and folding his arms across his chest.

"Too nice! Too nice!" Delesta parroted. "Lord, the male ego! He thinks that brushing his teeth before sex is too nice. Sweet Jesus, where does he get off with that? There is no such thing as being too nice. Anyway, I deserve nice. I've worked my fingers to the bone by cooking, cleaning, taking care of the kids, and paying the bills. Every night after work, he sits in front of the TV. Every weekend, all weekend, he's plopped in front of the TV. The only time it changes is when he cuts the grass, rakes leaves, or shovels snow, and even then he acts like he should get a gold medal for doing it. Spare me!"

"Spare her! Spare me!" bellowed Sanders. "A man's gotta have respect in his own house. Now, she may be careful 'bout what she says out loud, but I'm no dummy! I can read her eyes. I take a lot of bullshit out there to earn a buck and get along with The Man, but I'll be dammed if I'm going to put up with bullshit in my own house. And I don't see how she gets off thinking she's so perfect. Run a finger over my bureau or the blinds, and you'll see dust bunnies that've made themselves a right comfortable home. And cooking? Ha! Let me tell you. She used to cook me fried chicken, collard greens and corn bread. Now all I get is baked potatoes, broiled fish and salad. Health be damned! Life's too short, and I mean to enjoy my food. I deserve better."

"Let me ask you this, Doctor," said Delesta quietly. "If I disrespected him, would I work so hard to keep him healthy? Humph! No, I'd go on packing his arteries with grease and cholesterol till they pop. Then I'd sit back and party with the insurance money and the pension after I planted him six feet under. He ignores me and my needs completely. He won't listen when I try to tell him something important, like how I feel. I've talked sweet and low for too long with no result at all. It's like speaking to a damn brick wall!"

Delesta sobbed. Franklin handed her the tissue box. Sanders patted her shoulder.

His ex-wife's voice rang in his thoughts, echoing Delesta. He flinched inwardly. Marceline had told him pretty much the same thing—demanding to know why he wouldn't listen to her concerns or consider how she felt and asking why his answer to everything was fear for how other people would judge them. He could almost hear her protesting against his insistence that how they lived their lives was important for the uplift of the Black community.

"Frank, I can't carry the history of our people on my shoulders, and I don't care what anyone else thinks. They don't live in my house or sleep in my bed. You do. You're supposed to be my best friend, not my shrink. Talking to you is like talking to a damn brick wall." And then she'd run sobbing into the bedroom and locked the door.

Sanders cleared his throat and snapped Franklin back to the present. "Listen, Dr. Rutledge, my wife has a good heart and I love her, but she is way off base. I mean, things need to be a certain way, and when we accept our place in the world without complaining, we can all be happy. If you believe in God, then you'll understand what I'm tryin' to say here. See, the way I learned it was that God is up here." Sanders's hand rose above his head. "Man is 'bout here." His hand touched the bridge of his nose. "And women are 'bout here." He placed his hand over his heart. "Now, I'm supposed to obey and serve God, and my wife is supposed to obey and serve me."

"Oh, no." Delesta's voice rose an octave as she pointed her finger at her husband. "Don't pull that old serve and obey chestnut! We're not living in the Middle Ages." She turned to

Franklin and said, "Whenever he's in a tight spot, he pulls out Bible stuff." She huffed, sat back, and crossed her arms.

Franklin's discomfort deepened. Hadn't he, like Sanders, expected Marceline to accept him as head of the household? Hadn't he tried to convince her that his way would guarantee them a life of domestic, social and professional perfection? Hadn't he told himself that Marceline's work as a teacher and artist was not as important as his?

These thoughts made him wince. He squirmed in his seat, took a deep breath, and returned his attention to the Hobsons. He caught Sanders looking at him in a no-nonsense, man-to-man sort of way.

"That's what I learned from my father, and if it was good enough for him, it's good enough for me. And while we're on the subject, let me point out that she spends way too much time with them Monday-through-Friday church meetin's, and come Sunday, why, she's in church all day. What do I work for? I work for my family. And when I come home, I'm hoping for bright lights, warm smells in the kitchen, a clean house, and a wife who is waiting for me with a smile on her face. Is that too much for a man to ask?"

"It might not be too much to ask if he'd sit and talk and listen to what happened in my day," said Delesta, wiping away the last of her tears. "It might not be too much to ask if he'd lift a finger every now and then to help out around the house. It might not be too much to ask if he'd talk about something other than his job or sports. But no, it's a peck on the lips; eat in silence; belch, fart and grunt; and then bury himself in front of the TV. The way I see it, if he wants someone to keep the house spotless, he can either do it himself or hire a maid. I'm a flesh-and-blood woman. I have needs, and they aren't about dishwater and dust rags!"

Franklin cringed. He had complained bitterly about Marceline's outside interests, the dust on the furniture, and the dishes in the sink. He'd tried to get her to see how important order and cleanliness was to him. Marceline said she was doing her best, but what with work and their social engagements, she had to set priorities and take time for herself. If he didn't like dust and dirty dishes, he could goddamn well dust the furniture himself and put the goddamn dishes in the goddamn dishwasher. And that led to him lecturing her about cursing, which did not go well at all.

"You see how emotional she is?" said Sanders. "I keep a roof over her head and food in the fridge. That's what a man's supposed to do. And this is the thanks I get? It's intolerable, and I'm not gonna sit here and be verbally abused. I've got nothin' to be ashamed of, and what I deserve is my propers. I'd like to hear what she has to say about that!"

"Well," said Delesta, hands on hips, her head beginning to wag. Franklin held his breath, praying she would not remove her earrings. The last thing he wanted to do today was break up a physical altercation between his clients. Delesta left her earrings on, but in a stern voice, she said, "Let me tell you what about that. He don't hear his propers when they come right at him. Proper is as proper does. Even if I'm not home, his dinner is on the table at the time he wants it. The bed is made, and the kitchen is clean. This isn't about what's done or not done. This is about control. He wants to control my time and my activity. He has a problem with anything I do that's not directly tied to his comfort. I can't stand it anymore!" She burst into tears a second time.

Again, Franklin's thoughts spun back to something Marceline had said. "You ask me how I feel, and if I tell you the truth, it completely blows any chance we have for a tension-free evening. When I tell you what I really feel, you chastise, challenge and lecture me about my role as a Black woman and what I need to do to fulfill some image you have in your head of me as your wife. I can't trust you with my feelings because you don't listen to me. You don't see me!"

He hadn't understood what she'd meant by that. He'd always thought of her as the perfect woman, who just needed a bit of coaching on how to present herself as part of a perfect couple. Marceline was a talented sculptor, a graduate of Spelman. Her family pedigree was a classic example of W. E. B. Du Bois's "Talented Tenth." He had chosen and courted her for those reasons. In his mind, they made a perfect couple, and he was always proud to show her off. But suddenly, that didn't sound quite right. His uneasiness deepened.

"Dr. Rutledge," asked Delesta, "why can't you tell him how wrong he is? You're the expert, aren't you? Go on, tell him."

"How wrong I am? Well ain't that some nerve! I thought you'd jump right in and tell her how lucky she is to have a man like me. She can't do any better and she knows it. Good men are hard to find. She got one, so you go on and tell her that!"

Franklin had tried to tell Marceline how wrong she was, that he only had their best interests at heart. He had their whole future mapped out. It would be good for both of them. Why couldn't she see that? A glimmer of understanding dawned as he recalled the last thing Marceline had said before she left. "Frank, there are three marriages in every legal wedded relationship: yours, mine and ours. You still have yours. You've made it very clear what that is and what you expect. My marriage is over. I do not, cannot and will not fit into that tight, limiting prison of a life. And at this moment, our marriage is only a legal piece of paper, but my lawyer will take care of that." And then, she was gone.

Distracted by his memories and wearied by the Hobsons' bickering, he was relieved to see the session was over. Franklin breathed a sigh of relief and leaned forward. "I'm going to stop here because our time is up. There's a lot going on in your relationship. I'm going to suggest a series of sessions, let's say four to start. I'll be able to make some recommendations after I get to know you both better."

"Know us better?" said Delesta. "How much more do you need to know? I sat here and spilled my guts, and all the feedback I get is that you've got to get to know us better? Humph! I hired you. You work for us. I want service rendered for fees paid."

"You heard her," chimed in Sanders. "You need to tell us right now who's right and who's wrong!"

Franklin could feel a flush of irritation rise at the back of his neck, but he was an expert at keeping his emotions contained and constrained. He smiled. "Mr. and Mrs. Hobson, counseling doesn't work that way. I do not make judgments of right and wrong. But I can tell you this: You are both right, and you are both wrong. Name-calling and pointing fingers does not help. You are here because you think you have something worth saving. I can help you, but it's up to you."

A long silence ensued.

Sanders spoke first. "Okay, I'm willing if she is."

Delesta nodded her agreement.

They rose from their chairs, shook hands with Franklin, and left in silence.

The Hobsons had a lot of work to do, and next week they'd be back to do it. They'd sit directly in front of him with their feet on his oriental rug, their behinds on his brown leather couch, and their problems pushing hot air around the room. But there was an upside to their situation. They were both honest about their feelings, and they seemed willing to put in the effort to save their marriage.

Maybe, I wasn't honest about my feelings. I worked hard to present myself as calm and in control, even though I was never calm and I was clearly not in control of Marceline or our marriage, despite the fact that I wanted to be. Maybe this is one of the reasons my marriage failed.

The Hobsons' honest, loud, unfiltered emotions made him uncomfortable, but he admired their willingness to work on their relationship. He wondered why he hadn't put in more effort. Why had he given in, given up and let Marceline go without putting in the maximum effort? And what was he going to do about it now? Was there anything he could do?

Since the divorce, he and Marceline had spoken only a few times, to divide up possessions and deal with tax issues, bank accounts and legal payments. They had not exchanged anything personal. He thought about that as he wrote up his notes on today's session with the Hobsons.

Everything he'd done, every choice he'd made, was designed to bury his childhood experiences and memories of poverty, prejudice and rejection deeper and deeper into the past. And whenever they crept up, he'd done his level best to push them down again. Lately, they'd been pushing back hard and elbowing in on his personal and professional comfort.

Franklin put his head in his hands and took a deep breath. Of course the Hobsons' openness and honesty made him uncomfortable. They reminded him of problems in his own marriage. As often as Marceline had expressed her wants and needs—first, gently and rationally; then when ignored, loudly and insistently—he'd dismissed them as ego and a loss of perspective—just how Sanders had described Delesta.

He thought back to the last counseling session with Marceline and heard her words as clearly as if she were seated next to him right now. "The problem is," she'd told the counselor, "Franklin chose me the way he chooses his clothes, his profession, his car and everything else that makes him look upwardly mobile, like a reflection of perfection. I'm one of his props—part and parcel of a perfect package that'll take him to some far-off, perfect future. What I want and need simply doesn't enter the picture."

He didn't believe her assessment at the time, but now the truth of it smacked him in the head, pushed him back in the chair, and sat on him until he accepted it. His desire to prove himself and his worth as a human being had ignored her needs and infected their marriage.

And wasn't that Delesta's main complaint about Sanders?

The sudden awareness was a jolt to his mind and his heart as the truth woke up. His effort to control every aspect of his life was also the root of his unhappiness. As much as he wanted and needed to save other tortured souls, he realized he'd better do some deep work to save his own.

He did not hold out hope that this new understanding would, or could, lead to reconciliation, but he did want to clear the air. He wanted to tell Marceline that her reasons for ending the marriage were valid. He wanted to tell her how unfair he'd been and that he hadn't met her halfway in their struggle because he was stuck in an image of his marriage and not the reality of hers or theirs. He wanted to tell her that he loved her and to look deeply into her eyes and simply say "I'm sorry."

Guess Who's Coming to Dinner

Every family has its share of dysfunctional members, but sometimes we are the dysfunctional ones and don't even realize it.

I am not a happy camper.

The brightly colored plastic flags adorning the used-car dealership on Willis Street flap smartly in the brisk November breeze. As Clay and I pass Conticello's Market and turn left on Clifford Drive, a familiar row of old two-story homes comes into view. Tension twists my neck muscles into knots of Gordian proportions.

Clay stops at a white house with dark red trim. The bare hedges and naked maple tree in the front yard are stark evidence of winter's approach. The few leaves still clinging to its uppermost branches will probably fall before dark. I hope I'll fare better.

"Here you go, hon," Clay says. "Pick you up at six. Okay?"

"Clay, why wait till six?" My shoulders slump, and my stomach churns. "Take me home now. Spare me the agony."

"Now, Virgie. You know this is a second marriage for both of us. We agreed to split up this year so we don't have to navigate two dinners and two families in the same afternoon."

He's right. Together, we've had five years of blended holidays in all sorts of configurations with in-laws, out-laws, children and ex-spouses. But this is the first time I'll be alone with my family for a holiday since we got married.

Clay has done a wonderful job running interference between me and my family. It's one of the many reasons I love him.

My son, Fred, is hanging out with his friends. All of Clay's family, minus his mom who lives in Virginia, will be at Allen and Harrison's. They got married last year and want to show off their new house. Clay's son, Scotty; Scotty's wife, Maya; and their baby daughter, Sara, will be there too. Sara's birth makes me a step-grandmother, and I am still adjusting.

"I'll leave Allen's in time to pick you up at six sharp. Then we'll go home and lick each other's wounds, okay?" His eyebrows draw together and wriggle up and down—the "lust look." It never works. He looks too much like the Qantas Airways koala. I laugh.

"Okay." I kiss him and get out of the car but linger with my hand on the door.

"Virgie."

"Okay!"

Clay gives me a wink. I reluctantly close the door and watch him drive off.

Growing up in a small New England factory town has its charms: friendly neighbors; a slow, leisurely pace; and no need to lock doors. But it also has its demons, and I am about to have Thanksgiving dinner with several of them.

It's cold, and the sky is a dull, smoky gray. I walk up the steps and ring the bell. Mom opens the door.

"Hello, Virginia." She offers her cheek for my kiss but turns away before my lips reach it.

She heads down the hall to the kitchen. I follow, watching for signs of frailty. Mom is seventy-six and going strong.

Everything from her fig-brown skin and pink warm-up suit to the frizzled, gray wig on her head looks normal. If anything is missing, it's the mellowness that's supposed to come with age.

In the kitchen, Mom opens the oven to check on the turkey. Apparently satisfied, she closes the door and turns toward me. I steel myself for what will come next.

In school, it was "You have to study and get good grades." After college, it was "When are you going to find a husband, settle down, and give me some grandchildren?" After Fred was born, I divorced Lenny and went back to work. Then it was "Virginia, how can you leave your baby with strangers?" and "Lenny is a good man. I'll never understand why you divorced him."

Despite my best efforts, I always somehow failed to live up to her plan for my life, that is, until Clay. He charmed the scowl from her face before it could make an appearance. Since then, her comments have been focused on my hair, my outfit, or the size of my ass. I wait to see which one it will be today.

Instead, her left eyebrow lifts. "So, how's everything with you?"

Hmm, this is different. Dare I tell her I'm fed up with corporate life, that I'd love to quit tomorrow and write the novel that's been sitting in my head for the past five years? Do I tell her that Clay and I are thinking about selling our dream house and buying a condo to save money and help the boys pay off their college loans?

But none of that comes out. Instead, I say, "Okay, but I think I'm having a midlife crisis. I can't seem to—"

"Oh, I don't believe in this midlife crisis business, Virginia. I think one has to keep one's chin up and keep going. Most people give in to their feelings."

"Well, maybe, but I—"

"I've always kept a stiff upper lip. Why, your father never knew how devastated I was when he took our retirement money to bolster the liquor store." Mom moves to the counter and starts to savagely tear lettuce into a salad. "That was a terrible blow. I had to scrimp and save for years to make up for it. Yes, indeedy, a stiff upper lip is what's needed."

I bite my lip, which is anything but stiff, as my gut clenches.

"How's Fred?" Mom asks.

"He's fine, Mom."

"Why isn't he here?"

"He's hanging out with his friends today."

Her *humph* is followed by a *tsk*. "Does he have a steady girlfriend yet?"

"No, Ma. He and his friends still travel in packs. He's twenty-three. He's enjoying himself. I'm not going to worry about him until he turns thirty, and besides—"

"Thirty!" Her head shakes back and forth, and the gray wig wobbles. "Lordy, his best years will be gone. He'll be too old to start a proper family. Honestly!"

I grit my teeth.

"And you know he never calls." She tops the salad with honey-roasted pecans. "I'm not going to give him anything for Christmas. As a matter of fact, I'm not going to give anybody anything for Christmas. It's such a hollow holiday now, all the focus on stuff instead of substance. The holiday lights and sales start the day after Halloween! It never used to be that way. It's not worth it."

She puts the salad bowl to one side.

"And don't you get me anything, either. I have everything I need. Don't waste your money."

She brushes past me carrying a pan of Brown 'n Serve rolls.

"Can I do anything to help, Mom?"

"No, no, dear. You just sit and relax." Cupboard doors slam. Pots and pans rattle.

"Mom, are you sure I can't help you with something?"

"Yes, yes, of course! That's what I said, isn't it? I can handle this. It's all set, really."

I watch her for a moment, then wander into the dining room to check on the table. The newly polished silverware gleams. The gold-rimmed china plates sit proudly beside it. The glassware sparkles. Handmade paper place cards grace each setting. All our names are there, except for two. Dad died ten years ago, and Tamisha, my eight-year-old niece, died of a rare blood disease a year later.

Of course, Mom put Tony in Dad's chair at the head of the table. Tony, my pseudo-intellectual, Peter Pan brother, has been married and divorced three times. He's always peddling some foolproof scheme for making big money. Last year at Easter, it was the smoothie bar on Main Street. By Mother's Day, he wanted to open a consignment shop in the mall. At the Fourth of July picnic, he pitched a food truck franchise he planned to run from his basement. Tony's schemes depend on money, time and effort from everyone but him. When they fail to materialize, it's anybody's fault but his.

Junior, Tony's fourteen-year-old son, is on his right. Junior's mom is in a psychiatric hospital, and Junior blames Tony. Thandy, a musician who is also Tamisha's mom, was always a few cards short of a full deck, but Tamisha's death put her over the edge. Three months after the funeral, the police found Thandy wandering stark naked down Main Street, playing "God Bless the Child" on her saxophone and proclaiming the second coming of Billie Holiday. Tony had no choice. He had to put Thandy in the hospital.

Next to Junior is Chuckie, whose spirit is as pure as they come. He's a bundle of undiluted, four-year-old love-energy. Chuckie's mom is wife number three. When they divorced, Tony got Chuckie on weekends and alternate holidays. His ability to remain unscathed by the vagaries of his father's life amazes me.

Adrienne is on Mom's right. My younger sister lives her life as an empty journal waiting for an entry. The man she married wrote his own life story all over her—a depressing saga of mental and emotional pain whose ending is yet to be written. They're separated now, but he's trying to romance her back.

How someone like my sister managed to give birth to a steady flame of sanity like Sydney is beyond my understanding. My niece is seated between Adrienne and me.

Finally, on Mom's left is an extra setting with no place card. Huh?

The doorbell rings.

"Get that, will you, Virginia?" comes Mom's voice from the kitchen. "It must be Adrienne and Sydney."

It is.

Back in the kitchen, after our "Hi's" and "How've you been's," twelve-year-old Sydney scrunches her long-limbed, plus-size body into a chair and glues her eyes to her smartphone. Adrienne, deep in her victim phase, is dressed head-to-toe in black. She drapes herself on a stool by the breakfast bar and vents.

"I don't know if I should take him back or divorce him, Mom. He keeps saying how sorry he is about cheating on me, and he's been so sweet lately. He's even started taking Sydney out on father/daughter dates, but I—"

"Take him back," Mom says, one hand on her hip and the other pointing a large wooden spoon at Adrienne. "I know what I'm talking about. A woman needs a man. It's God's law. Take him back and make Jordan change his ways."

"But, Mom—"

"No 'buts' about it. Take him back. Try some new recipes. Get out of those baggy, black clothes. Put on some color, meet him at the door with a smile on your face and do whatever it takes to save your marriage."

Adrienne turns hopefully to me, but I can only manage a halfhearted smile. At least Mom's righteous advice is no longer directed toward me.

Mom bustles. She bastes the turkey, checks the corn pudding, stirs the ever-present collard greens, and vehemently refuses all offers of help. It's not a good time to ask about the extra place setting.

The doorbell rings again. It's Tony and the boys. I get a wet quickie kiss from Chuckie before he makes a beeline to the kitchen to sniff out a treat from his "Nana." Junior gives me a weak hug. Tony's eyes are unfocused. I can tell his thoughts are elsewhere, probably on his next big scheme. I give him cheek.

Soon, we're in the kitchen: Chuckie eating his treat, Junior and Sydney stuck like barnacles to their devices, and Adrienne in the middle of another complaint about Jordan. "I tried to talk to him about going to couple's counseling, but—"

"Counseling is a waste of time," says Mom. "It's all talk, talk, talk. And you know how I feel about airing private affairs in front of strangers. If you want your husband to act like the man you want him to be, you have to act like the wife he needs. Brush up on your womanly wiles." She grins and winks. "It always worked with your father."

Adrienne's face begins to crumple. Tony snatches the space between Mom's advice and Adrienne's oncoming tears to launch into his newest idea: flipping houses. "Listen, Virgie, it's foolproof. This town is bursting at the seams with run-down properties."

Mom watches Tony with her "no harm in indulging him" look. I steel myself for the pitch. "If you and Clay jump on this with me, we could be rolling in cash by next summer. I've got a list of prospects from the town clerk's office, and all I need is..."

I tune him out. I'm drained, exhausted, done. It's all I can do to stand in the doorway and watch. I can't listen to another word, not from Tony, not from Adrienne, not from Mom. Every holiday is identical. It's like we're caught in a time loop, reliving the same scene over and over. Nothing changes, not even the menu.

Mom samples the greens, smacks her lips, and looks at us with a twinkle in her eyes. "Guess who's coming to dinner?"

Intruder alert! Three pairs of black eyebrows shoot up, six brown eyes exchange quizzical glances, and three pairs of shoulders hunch. Thanksgiving dinners at our house are traditionally limited to spouses and children. Spouses, though not blood relatives, are tolerated as social necessities; dates, lovers and friends are actively discouraged, or at best received with frosty politeness. Who could have wormed their way into Mom's good graces?

"Merle is coming up to visit her brother in Hyannis," Mom says. "She's going to stop and see us on the way."

Merle Fontaine of the Philadelphia Fontaines is Mom's first cousin. I've always liked Merle. She's flamboyant, outrageous and classy. She has an infectiously upbeat attitude you can jump on and ride for miles. I cancel the intruder alert and relax. With Merle here, Mom will be on her best behavior, Adrienne will stop the "poor me" stories, and Tony will try to sell Merle on his latest scheme instead of hounding me for money.

The doorbell rings a third time.

"It's Merle!" Mom sings out. She drops the spoon she's been using to stir the greens. It clatters against the counter and hits the floor, but she doesn't even notice. She wipes her hands on her apron and trots off to get the door.

After she leaves, Adrienne reaches down, picks up the spoon, and huffs as she puts it in the sink. The three of us exchange another set of meaningful glances. Mom never acts like that when one of us is at the door. For a moment, we are united in collective gloom.

It isn't that Mom is uncaring. She's done the absolute best she could. She practically raised us by herself, holding down a full-time job as a salesclerk in a drugstore and managing the household alone. Dad was preoccupied with the liquor store and his golf game. Mom ran tired for years. We all knew what the deal was, and we all bear the scars: Tony's an irresponsible dreamer, Adrienne is a doormat, and I'm an obsessive overachiever.

Two sets of footsteps trip lightly down the hall to the kitchen. We pull out our company smiles to eclipse the sadness momentarily.

Merle doesn't walk into a room; she sweeps in, tall, thin and willowy. With a swift motion of one manicured hand, her mink coat leaves her shoulders, traces a graceful arc through the air, and lands on the stool next to Adrienne. Merle is wearing her signature color, cream, in the form of a lightweight wool pantsuit that clings to her slender curves. Her hair, colored a deep mahogany brown, is swept up in a classic ponytail, and the sparkle of her expensive jewelry pales before the twenty-four-karat joy in her eyes.

Her hugs, unlike those of my nuclear family, are close, tight and warm. *Maybe* she'll be the sponge that'll soak up the mess of this family, at least for today.

Mom is beaming. Adrienne absentmindedly strokes Merle's coat with a faraway look in her eyes. Tony gives off vibes like a mountain lion ready to stalk newly spotted prey. I cloak myself in forbearance and hope it will sustain me through the afternoon.

A few minutes later, dinner is ready. We sit in our designated seats. Tony says grace, then Mom fills our plates from steaming bowls and platters before passing them down the table. The kids dig in immediately.

Merle's face is animated. Her hands fly through the air, and she tosses her words in our direction. "Now, darlings," she says, "tell me what you've been up to. I'm dying to hear!"

Adrienne raises her head from her chest, gives Merle the 411 on Jordan, and with a question in her eyes asks, "Merle, what do you think about divorce?"

Uh-oh. Out of the corner of my eye, I see Tony's forkful of greens stop halfway to his mouth. I follow his gaze and see Mom's eyebrows meet in a sudden but short-lived frown. Our baby sister has just violated Mom's rule about airing dirty laundry.

Merle clucks her tongue. "Divorce is a funny thing, dear. It comes down to what you get and what they get to keep." She reaches across the table to cover Adrienne's hand with hers. "Now, here's the tricky part: what they must never get is your self-respect." She winks. "Sounds to me like you best leave him lay where the good Lord flung him and get on with your life!"

I watch Adrienne sit up a little straighter in her chair, with a firm set to her shoulders. Still, she looks Mom's way, as if seeking her approval of Merle's advice. Mom's smile does not reach her eyes as she says, "Marriage vows are sacred. The Bible says 'Till death do us part.'"

"Things change, Martha," Merle says softly.

"Not all things," Mom replies.

Tony jumps into the silence that follows. "I'm working on a business proposition to flip houses," he tells Merle. She turns to smile at him. Mom's eye twitches.

"It's foolproof. Run-down houses around here are a dime a dozen. They're crying out for someone to buy 'em cheap, fix 'em up, and sell 'em at a profit. I'm looking for investors." I watch him pause to see how his pitch lands. Tony is so predictable, it would be high comedy if it weren't so pathetic.

Merle calmly points out the positives—the certainty of making money if he does most of the work himself—and the negatives, like understanding that older homes often have serious code violations that will be expensive to fix.

Mom silently watches their exchange. I wait for Tony to ask Merle for money, but he doesn't. The smile on his lips is the first I've seen all day as he starts taking notes on his smartphone. He looks like a prize dog winning best of show.

"Excuse me," says Adrienne, getting up from the table. The look on her face tells me she's going to the bathroom for a private cry. I know she's unhappy, but she needs to suck it up, make a decision about Jordan one way or the other, and spare us the drama. I didn't drag my friends and family through a never-ending story when I divorced Lenny.

Sydney puts down her phone and says, "I made the honor roll."

"Honey, that's wonderful!" says Merle.

"And next week, I'm gonna try out for the cheerleading squad." She pauses. "But I won't make it.

"Why do you say that, sweetie?" asks Merle.

"Because..." Sydney chuckles. "I'm not skinny or blonde."

"Then why are you trying out?" I ask. "Is cheerleading something you really want to do?"

"I've got the moves for it, but honestly Aunt Virgie, I just wanna have some fun making those snotty stuck-up girls uncomfortable." I watch Sydney's eyes take on a wicked sparkle.

Tony smirks. Mom purses her lips. It's clear Sydney has gumption, but it might be misplaced.

As if she read my mind, Merle says, "I understand how you feel, Sydney, but let's think of a way to put your energy into something more productive."

"Whaddya mean?"

"Well, you're tall. You have long legs. I bet you'd do well on the basketball or track team. And you're smart. What about trying out for the debate team?"

"Hadn't thought about that but... but maybe I will." Sydney sits up a bit straighter momentarily proud of her height.

Junior and Chuckie sit mesmerized by Merle's glitter, chatter and charisma. She speaks to them on their level, no "my, how you've grown" stuff. She asks them about school, what they do in their spare time, and who their friends are. She pays attention to their answers. Junior's face relaxes as he tells Merle about his heavy metal band. They call themselves the Last Wave. Junior plays the drums. I did not know that. Chuckie tells Merle about his chess video game and how his favorite piece is the knight, "'Cause it looks like a horsey."

Eventually, even Mom's smile melts from Jack Frost winter to warm, sunny summer as she and Merle crack up over silly stuff they did as teenagers: sneaking cigarettes behind Uncle Bob's garage and playing spin the bottle with their male cousins in the basement during family reunions. "And," says Merle with a chuckle, "that one time we got wasted on bourbon from Aunt Helen's secret stash."

Mom listens to every word, unlike the constant interruptions I get when I try to tell her what's going on in my life. Adrienne pats Sydney's shoulder on the way to her seat. I glance over and can almost see wheels turning in her mind. I wonder if she's made a decision.

By the time Merle asks me about my life, the energy in the room is as light and airy as the whipped cream on Mom's pumpkin pie. I hear myself telling Merle about my troubles, but my mind has moved beyond my midlife muddle to what's happening in this room right now. Merle seems completely unaware of the effect she's had. She's getting everything I want to get from my family but can't.

My eyes watch while my mind calculates and questions "the paralysis of analysis," as Clay puts it. The usual family drama is nonexistent—no interruptions or unsolicited advice. No bickering. How is this happening? Why is it happening? And most of all, why can't it happen when it's just us?

With my mouth full of pie, I suddenly know. Merle isn't trying to get anything. She isn't trying to fix our problems or change us. She is just giving each of us her full attention and making thoughtful suggestions instead of telling us what we should do. Mom doesn't do that. I don't think Adrienne and Tony are even capable of doing it. And as much as I hate to admit it, I don't do it either!

My heart sinks. I put my fork down and sit stock-still as the hard truth hits full force. I've got as many "oughts," "shoulds" and "should nots" as Mom! The only difference is that she says hers out loud. Mine are silent but just as deadly. *Oh, my God. I'm one of the demons I've been complaining about!*

I'm surprised to feel shame... Shame for my mental put-downs and cynicism when dismissing Tony and his schemes before hearing him out or considering their potential; shame for tuning out Adrienne and her struggles without offering help, a listening ear, or a shoulder to cry on; and shame for not paying more attention to Sydney, Junior and Chuckie.

Mom starts to clear the dishes. Adrienne and I jump up to help. In the kitchen, we pour juice for the kids and make tea and coffee for us. I catch Adrienne's eye and smile.

Back at the table, I wonder what would happen if I listened, really listened to Mom's stories of stoic perseverance. What would happen if I really listened to Adrienne's "poor me" stories instead of thinking *Oh, God, here comes another one*? What would happen if I took a more active interest in what my niece and nephews are doing with their lives? What would happen if I really listened to Tony and heard his pain? Maybe nothing, maybe everything. But it might be worth a try.

I feel a rush of love for my slightly dysfunctional—but very normal—family. It fills me up and tunes me in, at least for this moment. I give thanks for the insight. It seems an appropriate thing to do on this day.

An hour later, amid hugs and goodbyes, Merle heads off for Cape Cod, leaving behind the scent of her perfume and seeds for healthy new growth in the bonds between my family and me.

At six sharp, Clay arrives to rescue me, except I no longer feel the need to be rescued. He notices the smile on my face as we walk to the car.

"What's up, cupcake?"

I tuck my arm through his as we walk.

"Clay," I say, hugging my new feelings close to my heart, "guess who came to dinner?"

Note: The original of this story first appeared in the 2021 edition of *The Connecticut Literary Anthology* and has been revised and expanded for this collection.

The Well-Wrapped Life

Dr. Franklin Rutledge thinks about Martha Rae Edmonds, a former client, as he prepares to deliver a lecture to college students majoring in psychology.

"Life's a gift, baby. Wrap yourself well!" This line from a commercial advertising the latest fashion trends describes Mrs. Martha Rae Edmonds to a T, and it's the first line of my upcoming talk to a group of psychology majors on the client-therapist relationship.

As I left the parking lot and started across campus to Webster Hall, I found myself reflecting on my connection with Mrs. Edmonds. She was seventy-seven years old when I met her. During our first session, I asked her how she would like her racial identity recorded and offered her the two most common terms—Black or African American. Mrs. Edmonds pressed her thin lips together and declared, "I'm not Black or African! I'm Brown, and I'm American!"

I asked her to tell me what she meant, and the response took up a full fifteen minutes of our first session. She was clear and adamant as she proclaimed that many African tribes had been complicit in the slave trade. And because names were changed and records either destroyed, poorly kept or nonexistent, there was no way she would ever know where her ancestors had come from.

Her eyes flashed in irritation at me as she added, "And even if I did know, what incentive would any African nation or tribe have to welcome me, what with the amount of White and Indigenous blood running through my veins?" She sucked her teeth and finished with a strong "Humph!"

I carefully kept my face neutral as I checked the "two or more" box on my racial identity form. I understood her view, perhaps even shared it to a degree, but what I needed to begin the therapeutic process was to understand why she'd come to see me.

As a young therapist, my approach had been to get to the heart of the problem as quickly as possible and use my professional knowledge to "fix" people. I had a bad case of savioritis back then.

It took time, several failures and more than a few therapy sessions of my own before I replaced "fix" with "heal." I also came to realize how much I could learn about my own issues as I helped my clients with theirs.

I asked Mrs. Edmonds to tell me more about herself. I learned she was widowed with three children, Virginia, Adrienne and Tony, and four grandchildren, three living and one deceased. After her husband's death eleven years ago, she'd stopped taking the bus and got her license in order to drive his green Ford Escort. Then she ran for and won a seat on the town's board of education. She'd campaigned the old-fashioned way: going door-to-door in the neighborhoods and stopping in the bars and restaurants in town to shake hands and pass out flyers. After her term ended, she was appointed municipal historian.

In her new position, she'd wrapped herself in her love of history and words by spending hours in the town library poring over old books, documents and records. She excitedly told me about the finds she'd uncovered. Her finds became notes, the notes became drafts, and the drafts became brochures about our town's founding and history. There followed awards and an honorary Doctorate in Humane Letters from Greenwood College.

As she listed her accomplishments, her face became animated—an arched, well-shaped eyebrow and a self-satisfied smile accompanied each one. As her smiles grew wider, her lips parted to reveal a partial gold cap on her right front tooth. She spoke with gusto, relish and perfect diction.

Of course, I complimented her on her successes. And my compliments were genuine; I was impressed by her energy and drive, two qualities we shared. I too had a list of professional accomplishments: awards, honorary degrees and important board positions. On paper, we were both successful. But appearances on paper often do not match the truth of the lives they portray.

I took the next step to dig beneath her polished surface. I crossed my legs, leaned forward and asked, "Mrs. Edmonds, what brings you to therapy?"

She sat back, took in a deep breath, and let it out. Silence followed, filling the room and sitting between us.

I never break these moments. It's important to let the client find their voice, and they eventually do.

Finally she said, "Well, Dr. Rutledge, I'm not a fan of talking about private matters to strangers. Never have been. And I certainly don't want to talk about my issues with my children, especially with the way things are now."

"And what way is that?" I asked softly.

"Things are changing between us." She paused. "You see, I always wanted my children to be happy, so I did what mothers do. I pushed, prodded, suggested and, if I'm honest, criticized. I… I—" She stopped and shook her head.

"And?" I urged.

She looked at me and sighed. “My son’s life is a mess. He dropped out of college, divorced three times, can’t keep a job for more than a few months, and is always coming up with get-rich-quick schemes that never pan out. I don’t know how he pays the rent and keeps the lights on, but he is a good father and his boys seem happy.”

“And your relationship with your daughters?”

“Until last year, pretty grim. One is divorced and remarried, and the other is in an unhappy marriage to a totally unsuitable man but can’t seem to get it together enough to either stay or leave. They always ignored all my advice and clearly resented me giving it to them, but after Thanksgiving last year things started to change.”

“In what way?”

Her eyes brightened. “At Christmas, Virginia and Adrienne asked me to give them our family recipes and show how to make them. They said they would alternate family dinners between them to help out and give me a break. I resisted, but they insisted. And frankly I was relieved. I’ve always done the cooking, but honestly it was getting harder every year to do it all.”

“Could you have asked them to help you do the cooking at your home?”

Mrs. Edmonds shook her head. “Uh, no. There can be only one cook in my kitchen and that’s me. Now, don’t get me wrong, I still have to put my two cents in once in a while, but they’re doing all right. Now I have more time to think, and I’ve been thinking more about me and... Well, you see, my time, like yours and everyone else’s, is running out.” She sat back, crossed her legs, and looked me in the eye. “I do not want to meet my maker dragging a passel of demons along with me. I need to tie up the loose ends of my life. That’s why I’m here.”

This was what I’d been waiting to find out. It was clear Mrs. Edmonds was ready to allow herself to enter a client-therapist relationship that did not carry judgments.

Judgment. This was another difficult lesson I'd had to learn. I was guilty of judging many of my clients, and often still do, but I've learned the importance of keeping it to a minimum and checking myself when I do it. It's a constant dance. I'm always learning new steps. And depending on the client, it can be difficult not to judge, especially if one happens to be self-judgmental.

I was and often still am hard on myself. I came to see this as another characteristic I shared with Mrs. Edmonds. Honestly, the more I listened to her, the more she reminded me of myself. I'm sure that's one reason our time together left such a strong impression on me.

When I asked how she chose me to be her therapist, she smiled mischievously.

"Six degrees of separation, Dr. Rutledge. Well, it's six degrees of separation most places, but in this town it's more like one or two. You see, my daughter Virginia knows your former wife, who recommended you. And it's rather comforting to know that if I'm going to talk to a stranger, at least it's a stranger who's known to someone I know."

Marceline! My heart shrinks a bit every time I think about my divorce—or rather her divorce, since she divorced me. As an unwilling ex-husband, I'm still struggling to come to grips with my sadness and sorrow, even though I now understand her reasons for divorcing me.

Like Mrs. Edmonds's expectations for her children, I had expectations for my marriage. And like Mrs. Edmonds, I pushed, prodded and even criticized to convince Marceline to be what I wanted her to be, instead of accepting her for who she was. Marceline never shared my expectations of her or for us.

I pushed that memory aside and returned my attention to the woman in front of me. Although Mrs. Edmonds appeared strong and resilient, she was also vulnerable. For many reasons, she had waited a long time to wrap herself in a life of her own making, I think largely because most of her earlier wrappings were made for her. She, like me, was born in the South. She'd had to deal with all that meant for Black folks trying to get by and "make a way out of no way," as the saying goes.

Her father left shortly after her birth. Her mother died when she was three, and she was sent north to be raised in the authoritarian household of an aunt and uncle at a time when society did not care what a woman might want outside of husband, home and children. Except for Black women, of course, who were expected to do it all—bring home the bacon, fry it up in the pan, manage the household, and pamper the man.

Mrs. Edmonds learned the lesson well and sang that song for the next fifty years. She'd graduated secretarial school at the top of her class, but unable to find a job in that field, instead ended up working as a salesclerk in a drugstore, all while keeping house, being a wife and a mother to three children, and handling the legal and financial responsibilities of the household.

Underneath those outer wrappings, Martha Rae Edmonds hid her vulnerability along with her demons. And she did have demons, though until now she'd been reluctant to face them, trace them or erase them.

However, she was, as I learned over our time together, an expert in sniffing them out. She'd let them raise their eyes from her subconscious mind and open their mouths to speak. Then she would smash the lid of defiance, dismissal and denial on top of their heads.

Did that work for her in the long term? Sadly, no, because despite Mrs. Edmonds's glowing community and social success, her wrappings had started to come apart at the seams and experienced more than a few rips and frayed edges. The demons boldly peeked out over the brave toss of her head, the flick of her hand, and the smile on her lips that never quite reached her eyes.

Mrs. Edmonds and I met weekly over the next several months. As she began to trust me, she allowed the demons to tiptoe up and out. One by one, they fell from her lips to my ears and my notepad.

Her mouth would tighten as she expressed anger at the father who'd left, moved to Oklahoma, and started a new family. She explored the crushing hurt that he'd visited her only once, on her twelfth birthday, and that she had two half-siblings she'd never met.

She shared her sadness at losing her mother and her fear at leaving the South and moving north to live with an aunt and uncle she hardly knew. "It was hard living under their rules," she said. "Uncle insisted that I read the newspaper to him every morning, and he would correct my diction and pronunciation over and over until I lost my southern accent."

She described her aunt as a harsh taskmistress who insisted her free time be spent working in the garden, chicken coops and kitchen. "I felt like a servant. But thanks to them, I learned to speak the King's English and run a tight household."

Her shoulders drooped as she talked about the utter exhaustion she'd experienced working a day job and coming home to what she described as her "third shift"—taking care of her husband, her children, her house and her church activities.

She teared up as she told me of the grief she felt when her grandchild, Tony's daughter, Tamisha, died at age eight from a rare blood disease.

My job as her therapist was to create a safe space, listen to her pain, and respond with empathy and warmth to show I understood what she was feeling. It wasn't hard. Our shared southern background and need to be in control to ward off vulnerability gave us solid points of connection that transcended gender and age. I listened and passed her the box of tissues when necessary. I understood her because I was learning to understand myself.

When the last demon was outed, she paused, looked at me, cocked her head, and shrugged her shoulders. "Not a pretty picture, is it?"

She may have seen things that way, but what I saw was the gift of a woman who'd faced her demons and was wrestling them to the ground. I saw a woman no longer hiding under the superficial trappings of awards, fame, fashion and family perfection; a woman newly wrapped in honesty, strength and resilience.

Watching her progress over our time together, I could not help but think about my own. I was still wrestling with my demons of privilege, perfectionism and social status, acknowledging how they'd driven me most of my adult life, how they'd driven away the woman I loved and ended my marriage. I'm still sorting things out and making amends. I'm not sure Marceline and I can ever reconcile, but we are talking and establishing a genuine friendship. That's progress.

One crisp fall day several months later, Mrs. Edmonds walked through my office door, took her place on the couch, and folded her hands in her lap. She was clear, firm, formal and deliberate. "Dr. Rutledge, I want to thank you for your help, but the time has come to terminate our sessions."

She watched my face for a reaction and got none. But she did get the question I always ask in moments like this.

"Are you sure?"

"Yes," she replied with a nod.

I followed with the next question recommended by protocol. "Have your goals been met, or is there another reason you care to share with me?"

"Well, Dr. Rutledge, if all my goals were met, my son would hold down a good job and stop pestering the family to invest in his schemes, Virginia would call me more than once a week to check in, Adrienne would find a way to make her marriage work, and I'd be able to locate and meet my missing siblings if they are still alive."

She looked at me. I looked back, keeping my face neutral.

"None of those things have happened, but I have forgiven my father for abandoning me. I've made peace with losing my mother, my husband and Tamisha. I have a more accepting and realistic view of my childhood with my aunt and uncle. They did their best, and I'm doing mine. I've softened my expectations of how my children should live their lives. And as a result, we are slowly growing closer."

Her face softened. "I'm in a place where I can move forward with a bit more ease. I've learned that nothing is perfect." She grinned, her gold cap sparkling. "Not even me." She leaned forward. "I never thought I'd be able to do this kind of work, but I did, and it's because of you. Thank you, Dr. Rutledge."

Ending therapy sessions is always a mixed bag. Some clients leave to seek another therapist or another type of therapy, or because they just need a break. Others feel I'm not challenging them enough, or that I'm challenging them too much. Some can't afford the cost. Others, like Mrs. Edmonds, feel they've gone about as far as they can in the therapeutic process. And so we parted. I was sad to see her go, but she was ready. I wanted to give her a hug but felt it might be taken the wrong way. She must have sensed my unexpressed desire for she patted my cheek as she left.

I like to think Mrs. Edmonds no longer saw me as a stranger but as a friend and fellow traveler on the road to making peace with life. She may have come to therapy to heal her anger, sadness and disappointments, but as much as I helped her, she also helped me. We both grew from our work together.

Nine months after our sessions ended, Virginia called to tell me that her mother had passed away in her sleep. I was saddened to learn that but confident that Mrs. Martha Rae Edmonds had met her maker with a calm heart, clear mind and clean slate. I still think of her fondly, and her well-wrapped life continues to inspire mine.

After Professor Ortiz introduced me to his class, I walked up to the podium in Webster Hall with the memory of Martha Rae Edmonds sitting comfortably on my shoulders and in my heart. I looked out over those young faces and opened my lecture with "Life's a gift, baby. Wrap yourself well!"

Warrior Women of the Third Sunday

Book clubs have been around for years. In addition to reading and discussing books, they form a foundation for friendship and sharing. This story is based on my own book club, which has been meeting since the 1980s. Membership shifts and lives change, but the Warrior Women of the Third Sunday still read, meet and dish.

"Warrior Women of the Third Sunday." That's what we call ourselves. Shortly after we formed the group, Cheryl, in a burst of inspiration, wrote a poem. It's a poem with strong, deep, nourishing images, referring to us as wise warriors, the women of the third Sunday. She read it at last December's meeting: a Christmas present from her to us. We all clamored for copies, and the Warrior Women of the Third Sunday is now who we are.

I think the poem hit home because the words conjure up a feeling of power and strength that bursts out when we come together to recognize and celebrate ourselves, like our aunts, mothers, grandmothers and ancestors did before us. They did it while gathering water at the river, planting crops in the fields, sewing quilts, or helping each other at weddings, births and funerals. We do it over books, tea and talk on the third Sunday of every month from 3:00 to 5:00 p.m.

Our meetings are a lot like a buffet—lots of variety. You can sample a little bit of everything and go back for seconds if you want them. We start with a book, poem or piece of music, and once the entrée of choice has been sliced, diced, chewed, reviewed and digested, we move on to the side dishes of our lives.

Marceline, a college art professor, is in charge of this month's program. She chose a *New York Times* bestseller, *The Adventures of Portia Lovely*, by Sonya Taylor. It's about a twelve-year-old girl who runs away from home on a magical journey with three imaginary friends.

One by one they arrive, our Warrior Women of the Third Sunday. Ardell and Connie enter laughing. They are lifelong buddies, godmothers to each other's children, and keepers of each other's secrets. Connie joined us last year, after her airline transferred her here. Nicole, a lawyer, is thinking about getting a divorce. Georgia, a lieutenant in the fire department, was born in that state and named after it. She's widowed and raising her grandchildren. Pat's a city planner. Leola works for Marceline's ex-husband. She played go-between during the divorce and they kept in touch afterward. Eventually, Marceline invited her to join us. Frankie is a school social worker married to Johnny, a cop. And I round out the group, running the marketing department at a utility company.

The last one to arrive is Claudette. She quit her corporate job to open an event planning business and craft supply store. Cheryl's not here because she and her husband are on vacation in Greece. Neither is Mariposa. *I wonder if that means...?*

Marceline answers my unspoken question. "Mariposa is on an archaeological dig in Peru."

Picture nine open mouths.

"Get out!" screams Ardell.

"Yep!" says Marceline. "She got a big grant and took off last week. She'll be there for three months."

The room fills with whoops and hollers of "You go, girl!" and "Well, all right!"

"How did her husband handle it?" I ask.

"Bob's planning to take the kids out of school and join her for a couple of weeks. Says he's proud of her, wants to be a part of her new adventure, and thinks it will be excellent cultural exposure for the kids."

"Any other announcements or updates?" Marceline pauses and looks around the room at each of us. "No? Okay, let's talk about Portia. I think the real meaning of the book is symbolic," she says. "Portia's journey is like the seven stages of personal growth: leaving home, learning to deal with relationships, developing self-esteem, getting in touch with emotions, being creative, defining your values, and getting right with the universe so you can come home to yourself. What do the rest of you think?"

"Girl, please! It's a children's book," says Connie. "Let your brain rest a minute, Marceline. Don't go so deep."

I jump in because I agree with Marceline. "You can read it both ways, you know. Kids love it. Portia's smart and has plenty of attitude. Clarence, the nearsighted seagull, is sweet and funny. Tasha the dog is brave. Horse-With-No-Name works magic on the bumps in the road. And all of us big kids can see the stages Marceline saw, so it's a twofer."

"Oo-o-o! I think you nailed it, Virgie." Nicole crosses her slender legs and brushes a few strands of hair from her face. Her hazel eyes seem pensive. She says, "I'm thinking about the stage I'm going through right now. Y'know, I went from home to college to marriage without ever living on my own. Do y'all think getting a divorce is like an adventure? I'd be leaving home, just like Portia."

Georgia is the first one to answer. "Could be. Maybe that's why this is so scary for you. You might be bumpin' into a couple of them stages all at the same time."

We laugh, but we can feel Nicole's pain. Several of us have, as the saying goes, been there and done that.

"If I go through with the divorce or take another shot at saving this marriage, I'm gonna take my mother's advice to heart for sure."

"What advice is that?" asks Ardell.

"Well... On my wedding day, Momma gave me her 'rules of marriage for women.' There are four." Nicole sits up straight and her white silk blouse ripples. Her gold bracelets jingle as she counts off her mother's Rules of Marriage on long slender fingers with perfectly polished nails.

"One, always have your own money. Two, never give up your women friends. Three, it's a mistake to tell him everything; keep some mystery about you. Four, whatever you start on day one, you'll have to do for the duration—so be careful."

"Well," says Leola, "why didn't you follow them?"

"They came too late. Greg and I lived together for a year before we got married. If she'd given them to me before we moved in, it would have helped, but she didn't approve. Said we were living in sin. So by the time Greg and I got married, the cake was baked. Things were okay while we lived together, but getting married changed something that I'm still trying to sort out. All of a sudden, I wasn't me anymore. I was part of him and he took up all the space in our condo. I want to know why men say 'I do' in the ceremony and then spend most of the marriage saying 'I don't.' Like, 'I don't like my shirts starched,' 'I don't eat casseroles,' 'I don't go out on Friday nights,' 'I don't like museums,' and 'I don't like you hanging out with your friends so much.'"

Marceline nods sympathetically. The rest of the room roars with laughter. But Nicole's face does not crack a smile. She plows on. "Wait! I'm not finished." She looks grim. "Now, the bride says 'I do,' and she mostly does. She does the cooking, the cleaning and the laundry. She works, does the dishes, has the kids, runs herself ragged in the process, and gives up a whole lot of who she is to make Mr. I-Don't happy. How come? It's not fair!" Her face is a storm cloud about to burst wide open.

Marceline looks pensive. Her divorce from Franklin happened a few years ago, but we know those wounds are still fresh.

"Honey," says Georgia, "if we knew the answer and followed rule number one, I wouldn't be driving a Hyundai, and the rest of these sisters would be in Jags!" We roar some more. A faint smile appears on Nicole's lips, and she joins in the laughter. "Thank God you aren't imaginary friends like the ones Portia has."

"That's something I've never been accused of!" hollers Frankie. She grew up knowing how to fish, farm and shoot. Last year, we spent one meeting talking about our treasures—people or things that changed our lives in some way—and Frankie had talked about her Uncle Buck. He'd taught her to shoot straight and true and made her promise she would always protect herself. After she finished the story, she reached into her purse and pulled out a Smith & Wesson.

Well, it got so quiet you could've heard a rat piss on cotton. The grapevine being what it is, her story eventually traveled to the ears of two men on the Citizen's Committee for Education. Frankie spent much of her free time working with them, and the experience was frustrating at best—her ideas were challenged at every step. Now, all of a sudden, the men turned charming. It took her a while to figure out why. Turns out they knew about the gun in her Gucci! What a hoot!

"Well," says Marceline, "Where do we go from here? Any more thoughts on the book?"

"Book, schmook. I want to know what stage Virgie's in," says Claudette. She leans forward, cups her cheeks in her hands, places her elbows on her knees and waits for the answer.

"We-e-ell, I'd say I'm in the middle of moving from getting in touch with my emotions to finding a way to express them creatively. I'm fed up with corporate life, and I'd quit tomorrow, but Clay and I bought our dream house a few years ago and we're still helping our boys pay off their college loans. It seemed so perfect and right when we did it. Now both of us are stressed out and stuck. Talk about being between a rock and a hard place! Going through the 'change' is not helping. I'm managing to maintain some measure of sanity by working out. Otherwise, I don't know..."

Georgia asks if I'm on hormones.

"Yeah, I was for a while, but you know, that stuff was giving me serious indigestion, walking-the-floor-in-pain-at-2:00-a.m. indigestion. I tried to blame my job, my diet, Clay and life in general, but when it came right down to it, it was the hormones. So I'm off."

"Are you flashing?"

"Like a goddamn neon sign!"

They giggle, and I sigh. "I used to love turtleneck sweaters, you know? Soft, fluffy cashmere turtleneck sweaters. Now I can't wear anything heavier than cotton knit, and it better have buttons or a zipper that I can get to fast—and girl, you know those fans they keep in church?"

They knew. Most of us grew up in the church and had clear memories of watching the sisters sit, fan and shout "Amen!"

"Well, I have one by the bed, one in the kitchen, and a battery-operated one in my pocket book." I glance back and forth between Georgia and Claudette. "You two have been through this, right?"

They both nod.

"Well, I'm mostly through it," says Claudette. "I still flash and have night sweats from time to time, usually when I'm feeling stressed out."

"For me, its ancient history," says Georgia. "I have enough on my plate. Thankfully, menopause is one less thing I have to worry about."

Six years ago, Georgia's daughter-in-law died from a brain aneurysm. Her son remarried and relocated to the Middle East, where he works as an engineer. Everyone, including Georgia's new daughter-in-law, agreed that the Middle East was not the safest place to bring up American kids these days, so Georgia is raising her grandchildren until her son and his wife return to the States.

"Think of hot flashes as a power surge, honey. All you got to do is ride the wave and reap the harvest," Georgia says with a grin.

"Yep! It's the post-pause fearless 'zest' thing," says Claudette. "You get this flood of energy and feel abso-swear-by-God-lutely fearless! You do what you want when you want, give your opinion straight up without flinching or worrying about anybody's feelings, and wear any color or combination that strikes your fancy. I swear I feel better now than I did at twenty!"

"And you look better too, dahling!" Connie smiles.

"Thank you, my dear. I accept all compliments gratefully and fully, and ever since I promoted myself to 'free-tirement,' I'm riding that post-pause 'zest' wave right into my own business. So I can now tell that brown-eyed, flat-shoe groove goodbye."

That was a new one. "What groove?" I ask.

"The brown-eyed, flat-shoe groove. See, if you have blue eyes and wear high heels, no one asks you to answer the telephone or get coffee. You're supposed to sit around the office and look good. That's your real job. Howsomever, if you have brown eyes and wear flat shoes, you are expected to be super competent and fill in all the gaps that Miss Thang misses. Get it?"

We got it.

"Georgia, what stage are you in?" asks Ardell.

"Girl, with what I've been through in the past few years, what with my daughter-in-law dying and Manny re-marrying, moving overseas, and leaving the kids with me, you know I've had a time. I should've worn beige and stayed quiet like a good mother-in-law, but you know that's not my bag. So I go and open my big mouth, and now I'm raising two kids when I should be kickin' up my heels. Don't get me wrong. I love my grandkids. But power surge or not, this is more than a notion. I guess I'm trying my best to get right with God, 'cause him and me's had a major falling out behind all this mess. But life goes on and I got to go on with it. You know what I mean?"

"Sure do," says Pat. "I'm struggling with a couple of those stages myself. Last week, I made the decision to come out to my dad. It was the hardest thing I've ever done in my life, but I couldn't hold out any longer without stifling myself to death. It was either him or me. I guess I should be glad that my survival instinct is strong."

"Pat! Girl, you mean to say you've been sitting here quietly all afternoon with that on your chest?" Leola leans forward. "Give it here and get it off!"

Pat sighs. Everyone except her father already knew she was gay. She'd come out to us about six months ago. Pat's story reminded me of my brother-in-law, Allen. He'd been out for years and is now married to the love of his life. All is well, but it was a journey for the whole family.

Leola had known about Pat for years. As she put it, "Shit, girlfriend and I used to swap pacifiers. We've got a lot of water under the bridge, and this wave isn't strong enough to sweep our friendship out to sea!"

Pat's challenge was facing her father and telling him the truth. She'd finally done it, and we all silently, and not so silently, applauded her.

"It went better than I'd hoped, but he was so hurt. He kept saying, 'But you've been married! You have children.' I don't think he really gets it. He wants to fix me up with some guy from his lodge. Yuck! He thinks I've got a disease and sleeping with his version of Mr. Right is the cure. If it didn't hurt so much, it'd be pretty damn funny." The corners of her mouth take on a determined cast. "At least now, I can live my life openly and like what I see when I look in the mirror."

"It's good to like what you see there, that's for sure. I wish I did," says Leola. Her face and voice turn mournful, and Pat, quick to pick up the smallest cue from her friend, zoomed right in.

"Leola, I know that look. Are you talking about what I think you're talking about?"

Leola looks around the room. Her gaze takes in all of us at once. Then she says, "This group is like a rainbow, and when I'm here, I feel totally accepted. But 'out there'"—she gestures toward the window—"I'm always trying to feel the same way, but most times I can't get comfortable. It is a color thing. I was the darkest one in my family, and you know what that's about."

Just as we knew about church fans, we know that color all too often dictates how loved, accepted and affirmed you are in your family, in the world, and even within yourself—especially if you can't pass the brown paper bag test. It's like the old jump-rope rhyme we sang as kids:

If you're White, you're all right,
If you're Yellow, you're mellow,
If you're Brown, stick around,
If you're Black, go back.

All the civil rights legislation and diversity training in the world has not changed that attitude in Whites or Blacks, and women like Leola catch the brunt of it. I look at her smooth flawless skin, clear eyes, wide nose and full mouth. She wears her hair in short dreads that follow the line of a well-shaped head. She looks like a fantastically rendered Fulani sculpture.

It's ironic, I find myself thinking. Leola is beautiful but not in a supermodel way. Her beauty is solid, strong, deep and rich. It will not fade at the first wrinkle, will never dry out, or need a face-lift. "Black don't crack." It will serve her well for the rest of her life, gradually absorbing and then reflecting her character. And yet, she can't fully appreciate it because she sees herself with eyes that have been poisoned by the "never skinny enough, never White enough, never rich enough" virus—an illness of epidemic proportions with no cure in sight.

Connie speaks up. "Leola, girl, you best follow this rainbow, starting from Virgie over there at the end of the sofa, around the room to the pot of gold at your feet. Take the love you find and carry it home with you. It's from us to you, and when things get bad, you take out a bit and wear it on your heart like a good luck charm. Okay, hon?"

Leola tears up. So do Pat and Georgia. Our gatherings often get watery because we talk real and stuff comes up all the time.

"Thanks, Connie." Leola's gaze sweeps the room. "Thank you, everyone."

It's quiet for a moment, and none of us feels the need to break the silence. Then Nicole's sigh catches everyone's attention. Ardell speaks first. "Uh-huh, Miss Nicole. You're processing something over there. Gonna dish?"

"I was thinking about Greg. When I married him, I meant it to be for life, but I want a real relationship, not a struggle that won't quit. He's a total three-P!"

"And what," asks Ardell, "is a three-P?"

"Partner, project, problem. When I married him, he was my partner. Then, to work on the marriage, I had to see him as my project. And now he's a problem. Get it?"

We got it.

"Something about his slant on life and love ties me up in knots and makes me feel guilty as hell, but talking to y'all is so therapeutic!"

"How's your sex life?" Connie smirks.

"What?"

"Sex life. You know, the horizontal tango, the nasty, doing the do, making whoopee, the beast with two backs..."

"Okay. Okay! I know what you mean!" Nicole chuckled. "Right now, for him, sex is masturbating to porn on the internet. I'm shut down. I can't get close enough to him to self-start my furnace, and I'm done with mercy fucks."

The warriors get off another good belly laugh at that one.

"I don't know what to do anymore. I hate to see him so wound up in knots. Everything I try seems to backfire."

"You know," says Marceline, "you might try leaving him be for a while. I haven't yet met the woman who could save a man who's drowning emotionally. We can be water wings, but they have to learn how to swim on their own. I know that firsthand. You remember I left Franklin alone after our divorce? Well, it's only now that he's starting to come to terms with his own issues. In fact, he called just last week and said he needs to talk."

"Girl!" says Ardell. "Do you think the two of you will get back together?"

Marceline shrugs and looks pensive. "I don't know. He wants to clear the air and go for closure. I still care for him. I'm happy that he's come to this point. But I don't know what that means for the future."

Nicole sighs. "I know you're right, Marceline, but there is such a big space between knowing what to do and actually doing it."

"You'll figure it out," says Marceline, "and we're here to help. Well, we've gotten way off the subject here. I know it's hopeless to think we're going to get back to Portia Lovely and her adventure, so let me say that if life were fair, we'd have answers to all our problems by now. But it isn't. We've dished with the best of them today. It's time for dessert, so let's finish up and go home. I don't know about you all, but I have a hungry dog to feed."

"Who's got a copy of Cheryl's poem?" I ask. "I know one of you must have it tucked in the corner of your wallet, back-pack or bra."

They snicker.

At last, Marceline produces a copy from the back cover of her sketchpad. "Ready to hear Cheryl's poem?"

We all sit quietly while Marceline reads.

Warrior Women of the Third Sunday

by Cheryl Curtis

We are uniquely united
We warrior women
Of the third Sunday
We be
We be fierce
We be funny
We be nurturing
We be intellectual
We be divinely inspired
We are a powerful force
We weave spaces in places
Where we had been kept apart
Here and out there
Are they turning over in their graves?
We ask *though... we know*

We be wise
We be wary
We be down
We be glorious
We be inextricably connected
Women warriors
Of the third Sunday
We be ***palms***
We seductively sway against the forces
But we remain firmly rooted
We be...
Because we are
Uniquely united

The Devil Gets His Due

Selling one's soul to the devil for fame, fortune and riches has a long history in storytelling—one has only to think of "The Devil and Daniel Webster," a short story by Stephen Vincent Benét, or the legend of the famous blues guitarist Robert Johnson at the crossroads. Here's a twist on that theme.

Human error caused the problem at the Bethel African Methodist Episcopal Church. Two letters, instead of one, were sent from the bishop's office, and the destinies of four people were changed forever.

Although the devil couldn't take credit for the problem, he was, as always, keen to take advantage of it. So he scurried to Bethel to get up to no good, and perhaps collect a soul or two in the bargain.

The pot began to stir on the second Sunday in March as the Right Reverend Webster Lee Woods marched triumphantly down the aisle behind the Bethel AME church concert choir. His face beamed, and sweat poured down his cheeks from the effort. This was the longest walk his portly, red-robed body had taken since last Sunday, and the longest he'd take again until next Sunday. His chubby hands clapped in unison with the choir. His voice boomed with gusto. Webster Lee was a happy man.

With some effort, he mounted the steps to take his position behind the pulpit, a huge mahogany affair draped with purple cloth and surrounded by white lilies from Ezra Brown's greenhouse. The choir sang "I'll Fly Away," and their spirited voices shook the walls of the church. Webster Lee raised his hands heavenward, giving emphasis and definition to the last line of the song. His deep, mellow tones rang out. "Let us now raise our voices in prayer as we have raised them in song!"

Choir and congregation bowed their heads as Webster Lee prayed loudly and earnestly for God's blessing on those gathered here and there, near and far, present and departed.

Next came the announcements.

"Sister Long is pleased to announce the engagement of her daughter Melinda to James Marvin Getts III.

"The church sends get-well greetings to Brother Fenster, who is in the Cloud Hills Convalescent home.

"Brother Peterson and Sister Adams invite you to the Easter pageant and potluck supper planned by the deacon board for Saturday next. Please see either one for tickets."

He paused. The church sat breathless, waiting for confirmation of what they already knew.

"Brothers and sisters, as you know, our beloved Bethel is bursting at the seams, but help is on the way! Bishop Price is sending us an associate pastor to help birth a new, bigger, better Bethel. Let the church say 'amen!'"

The church said "Amen," and the choir burst into "Oh, Happy Day."

As the choir and congregation sang, Webster Lee reflected on his good fortune. He'd started out as an earnest, skinny twenty-year-old, a self-taught preacher from Fayetteville, Arkansas. Then Bishop Price saw the promise in him and took him under his wing. Now, four decades and a hundred and seventy-five pounds later, Webster Lee was preparing to welcome his own protégé. Together, they would build his legacy—a large, wealthy, productive church. Then Webster Lee would be able to retire to spend his remaining days on earth writing and teaching.

After the service, he hurried to the parsonage. Miss Geneva Boone, his housekeeper, served him a ham sandwich, a slice of warm peach cobbler, and a glass of cold lemonade while he waited in his study. The new associate pastor was scheduled to arrive at two o'clock. J. S. Garrett was the young man's name, a good solid name. Webster Lee nodded in approval.

"Reverend Woods?" Miss Boone stood at the door, a look of uncertainty on her face.

"Is he here?"

"Well, yes, but..."

"Don't keep him waiting, Miss Boone! Bring him in. Bring him in."

"But Reverend Woods, there is something, err, uh... you need to know first."

"Miss Boone, bring him in!"

She clamped her lips and stepped aside to let two people enter the room.

Webster Lee blinked in confusion.

Seeing his bafflement and stepping past her own, Miss Boone quickly made the introductions. "Reverend Woods, this is Jeremiah Stephen Garrett and Jaleesa Scott Garrett."

"Apparently, there has been some sort of mistake, Reverend Woods," said Jaleesa, who crossed the room to stand in front of Webster Lee's desk. A red silk suit hugged six feet of alluring curves. Lips and nails glistened a bright cherry red. She stood straight and sure on impossibly high red heels, and a three-feathered red straw hat capped her crisp, naturally curly hair. Her smooth velvety Black skin was flawless. Her slanted doe-like eyes widened, and her toothy smile flashed as she reached out to shake Webster Lee's hand.

Webster Lee felt his loins stir at the touch of the woman's hand in his. Jaleesa's smile widened.

The pot began a slow rolling boil. The devil grinned.

"We realized it ourselves a few moments ago," said Jeremiah. He was a tall, thin, thoughtful, coffee-bean-colored man with large soft eyes. "We both have letters from the bishop. It's all a bit peculiar." Jeremiah's slender hand grasped Webster Lee's in a gentle greeting.

Webster Lee struggled to regain his composure amid the whirl of confusion in his mind and the now insistent throb in the crotch of his neatly pressed preacher's pants. "Ah, yes. Ahem, err, um... Indeed."

He was shocked at his body's response to Jaleesa. He thought he was finished with such yearnings. When his beloved wife, Malveena, had died five years ago, a grief-stricken Webster Lee had put his passion away and turned all his energy to building his church.

His whirling mind spied his housekeeper, still standing in the doorway.

"Ah, Miss Boone, please take these good people to the dining room and give them something to eat. I must call the bishop right away."

Once they were gone, he took a series of deep breaths, picked up the phone, and dialed the bishop's number.

"Webster Lee," said Bishop Price, "I apologize for what happened. A computer error of some sort, but unfortunately I can offer no easy solution to the situation. My choice for the position was Jaleesa. I had no idea the church had another J. S. Garrett among its ministerial staff. But they are both qualified for the position. Why not try them out for a while and then decide? I will make sure the appropriate funds are put at your disposal for a period of three months. Good luck."

Webster Lee was dumbfounded. The bishop's first choice had been a woman? Thoroughly befuddled, he returned to the dining room to inform Jaleesa and Jeremiah of the bishop's proposal.

As he listened to Webster Lee speak, Jeremiah's eyes held a look of compassion. But Jaleesa's eyes also held a look. The only person to see that look and interpret it correctly was Miss Boone, and the sight put fear in her heart.

Geneva Boone had taken care of Webster Lee since Malveena's death. She was Geneva's best friend, and as Malveena lay dying from breast cancer, she exacted a promise that Geneva would look after Webster Lee. She kept her promise, and in the process of cooking, cleaning and keeping his pastoral schedule, the secret love that she held in her spinsterish bosom came to full bloom. Longing and devotion filled her heart and soul. It beamed out of her eyes, but Webster Lee never noticed. And Geneva Boone took an immediate dislike to Jaleesa.

The devil's grin widened.

The next day, Webster Lee devised a division of responsibilities for church functions. To Jaleesa, he gave fundraising, visiting the sick and shut-ins, the weekly bulletin, and new member recruitment. Jeremiah got the concert choir, Bible study groups, youth work, and pastoral counseling. But Jaleesa took one additional function upon herself, namely the rapid and complete seduction of the Right Reverend Webster Lee Woods.

It was subtle at first—looks, light touches, smiles and compliments. Webster Lee, absorbed in being fair and righteous but embarrassed about his body's unbidden reactions, ignored her advances. Jaleesa, not so easily put off, decided to up the ante.

One night after a supper of Miss Boone's hearty fried chicken, candied yams, homemade biscuits, collards and sweet potato pie, the four residents of the parsonage trooped upstairs to the second floor. Jaleesa bade them all goodnight and turned into the room across from Miss Boone. Jeremiah then went into his, which was two doors down from Jaleesa's, and Webster Lee continued on to his bedroom at the end of the hallway.

About an hour later, Jeremiah finished reading his Bible and knelt by his bed to pray. The squeak of a loose floorboard from the hall caught his attention. Next came a soft *tap, tap, tap,* followed by the squeaking hinges of a door opening and closing. In short order, mattress springs creaked as two people moaned in the throes of passion.

Jeremiah rushed to his door and looked out in time to meet the horrified eyes of Miss Boone, who stood in the hallway, looking at Webster Lee's room. Jeremiah watched as pain, fear and anger replaced her usual gleam of devotion.

He felt a bit of fear as well. He had believed he would be named associate pastor and had traveled a long way from Virginia for this, and an even longer way through his personal dark night of the soul. For the past fifteen years since coming north, Jeremiah had worked his way from church to church as discipleship pastor, youth pastor and worship pastor. Bethel, he'd thought, would be his next step on the way to pastoring his own church again, a reward for keeping his faith through storm and doubt.

Now, however, faced with the out-and-out fornication taking place down the hall and knowing the frailty of human character, Jeremiah felt the foundations of his faith crumble again.

The atmosphere in the parsonage changed overnight. Miss Boone was a woman scorned and a soul in torment. The quality of the meals went from delicious to dreadful. Webster Lee, caught between the needs of his spirit and the desires of his flesh, stopped eating altogether and began losing weight. Jeremiah, coveting the associate pastorship, began to feel less than kindly toward Jaleesa. And Jaleesa herself smiled the smile of a cat who has caught a mouse and knows exactly what to do with it.

The pot had come to a full boil. The devil sat back and gleefully waited.

When Miss Boone could take no more of what was going on under the very roof where her friend Malveena had lived for so long, she called the bishop and told him everything. Aghast, he agreed to come at once and have a talk with Webster Lee. He arrived the next day at 3 p.m.

That was when the pot boiled over and all hell broke loose.

Miss Boone marched Bishop Price into the study, expecting to find Webster Lee hard at work on next Sunday's sermon. Instead, there he was, lying naked on Malveena's white leather sofa with his eyes closed and a blissful look on his face. An equally naked Jaleesa sat astride him, a can of whipped cream in one hand and a bottle of chocolate syrup in the other. Webster Lee looked like a hot fudge sundae, only the cherry was missing. Jaleesa turned at the sound of two simultaneous gasps and said, "Uh-oh."

Webster Lee's eyes popped open to see the faces of Miss Boone and his bishop. His lips moved, but the only sounds that came out were choking, gasping and wheezing. His chest heaved and bucked so hard that Jaleesa was thrown to the floor in a shower of chocolate cream.

"Oh, my God!" hollered Miss Boone. "He's having an attack!"

Jaleesa jumped to her feet and shot back, "Well, don't stand there! Call 911!"

Recriminations and accusations were put on hold for the long, anxious moments during which the city's emergency medical team responded to the call and administered aspirin and nitroglycerin before bundling Webster Lee onto a stretcher and rushing him to the emergency room. There, Jeremiah joined Miss Boone, Jaleesa and the bishop in silent misery as they sat waiting for the doctors, hoping for the best but fearing the worst.

Fortunately, the best won out. Webster Lee had suffered a massive heart attack, but he would live. That much was certain. The doctors placed him in intensive care so they could monitor the damage to his heart tissue before making a prognosis for recovery. The bishop went to pray with Webster Lee and then informed Miss Boone, Jeremiah and Jaleesa that he wanted to see all of them in his office as soon as Webster Lee was released.

Webster Lee would recover. Relief flooded Geneva Boone. And in a heartbeat, she turned her pain, fear and anger toward Jaleesa.

"Hussy! See what you've done? Gone and near killed Webster Lee with your sneaking Jezebel ways. Sleeping your way into Bethel. I hope I live long enough to see the devil come take your evil hide!"

The devil rubbed his hands in anticipation.

Jaleesa pulled herself up to her full height and pounced back. "There is nothing evil about what we did, Miss Boone. Webster is a passionate man. I'm a passionate woman. I helped him remember what passionate people do. If making love helps me do God's work here, so much the better, but calling me names isn't going to get Webster out of the hospital any faster. Seems to me you'd do better to mind your own little red wagon instead of trying to ride around in someone else's. If you hadn't run your mouth to the bishop, Webster would be home sound asleep and satisfied, instead of lying here with wires and tubes coming out of who knows where."

Miss Boone was about to sputter more invective when Jeremiah interceded.

"Sisters! Sisters! Please! Don't make this situation any worse than it is. We could all do with a bit of God's grace on this awful night. Let's go home and pray for the rapid recovery of our dear brother."

They rode back to the parsonage in silence. Later that night, Jeremiah's internal struggle escalated as he wondered if his fall from grace had contributed to this mess.

The devil, sensing an opportunity, deepened Jeremiah's struggle. He whispered into Jeremiah's ear, telling him, "Wait until the bishop leaves, then tell the church elders about Jaleesa and Webster Lee's sin of fornication. You will be a shoo-in for the position."

Deep into the night, Jeremiah prayed and struggled while the devil whispered and cajoled.

Then, just before daybreak, Jeremiah came to a resolution. *That's it! I am to pastor. Maybe not at Bethel, but somewhere, there is a church for me. Not my will, Lord, but yours*, he prayed. His anguish faded, and he drifted into a peaceful sleep.

In disgust, the devil turned tail and rushed to the hospital to work on Webster Lee.

Later that morning, Jeremiah doubled his efforts to keep things running smoothly at church. He calmed and counseled the parishioners but kept the circumstances behind Webster Lee's illness to himself. Miss Boone, who did not want anyone to think badly of "her" reverend, did the same, but her mood turned dark. Jaleesa, her secret safe for the moment, got busy working the parish like a shrewd politician running against an incumbent.

A few days later, Webster Lee called for Jeremiah and told him, "Jeremiah, the devil's voice won't leave me be. He's been in my head every day, talking long and talking strong, telling me I can have a rich church, a bishop's position, and all the personal wealth I can handle. All I have to do is keep quiet about what's happened and convince everyone else to do the same. God help me, Jeremiah, it looked mighty good until I realized that I would die with a lie on my heart and go to hell for eternity. Life is short, Jeremiah, and eternity is long. When I am released from the hospital, I plan to confess all, apologize to the congregation and the bishop, retire and spend a year in contemplation. I will recommend you for the position of pastor of Bethel. Given the state of affairs, I'm sure the bishop will want to hold off assigning an associate pastor for some time. There is much healing to be done first."

Jeremiah, though excited and joyful, insisted Webster Lee get completely well before making a final decision.

The devil, seeing he had to give up on Jeremiah and Webster Lee, now turned his attention to Jaleesa and Miss Boone.

He found Miss Boone busily putting roots on Jaleesa. Ignoring her Christian adulthood, Miss Boone had returned to Vodou, the religion of her youth in Haiti. She chanted, mixed potions, and burned incense to such a degree even the devil was impressed. Finally, she fashioned a straw doll, dressed it in red, stuck pins all over it, and hung it by its neck from a three-penny nail she buried deep in Jaleesa's bedroom door.

When Jaleesa saw the doll, she yelped loud enough to wake the dead. She made a beeline for the stairs, searched the house for Miss Boone, and found her in Webster Lee's study, scrubbing chocolate stains out of Malveena's oriental carpet.

Without a word, Jaleesa tackled Miss Boone. Jeremiah, on his way back from choir practice, heard a fierce commotion in the study and tried to enter, but Jaleesa had locked the door behind her. Such a caterwauling and carrying on, he'd never encountered. The floor shook, the walls shook, the whole house shook. The air shimmered like lightning and vibrated like thunder. Then he heard a loud boom and a sucking sound, followed by sudden quiet.

Jeremiah tried the door again. This time it flew open at his touch. He rushed in to find the room in complete disarray, furniture out of place, lamps overturned, windows broken, books and papers everywhere, and Malveena's expensive oriental carpet ripped to shreds.

Jaleesa and Miss Boone stood grinning with their arms around each other's waists. They were staring into a huge smoking hole in the floor, a hole so deep it dropped through the basement into unfathomable darkness.

They tripped over each other's words as they tried to tell an incredulous Jeremiah what had happened.

"Well," said Jaleesa, "the devil popped up while Miss Boone and I were fighting..."

"Oh, he was impatient, insistent, triflin' and plain rude!" interrupted Miss Boone. "He offered Jaleesa the position of pastor and told me I could have Webster Lee in exchange for... for... for..." She paused and choked back her fury.

Jaleesa jumped in. "In exchange for our souls! Our souls! Well, when we heard that, we realized he'd been dogging all of us during this whole mess and..."

"The nerve!" sputtered Miss Boone.

"Indeed!" Jaleesa chimed in. "We knew what we had to do."

"We exchanged glances..." Miss Boone's eyes narrowed, "and without a word passing between us, took our hands off each other, and laid 'em on the devil."

"Oh, Brother Jeremiah," said Jaleesa. "You should have seen Miss Boone try to kick his natural behind into next Wednesday! It was a sight!"

"Then," said Miss Boone, "he got so angry and flustered, he stamped his foot hard enough that he... he..."

"Opened a hole in the floor," cried Jaleesa.

"So we pushed him in!" exclaimed Miss Boone. "He dropped into the hole and got sucked right back down to hell in a column of smoke and fire! That rascal got his just desserts for sure!"

And so did everyone else.

In time, Webster Lee made a full recovery. He accepted that his physical and sexual health were as important as his spiritual health and soon realized the solution to this new awareness had been in front of and beside him for years. He married Miss Boone and retired to Fayetteville, Arkansas.

Jeremiah became pastor of Bethel and is doing quite well with his brand of thoughtful, intelligent preaching.

Bishop Price, after consulting with Jeremiah and with the congregation's approval, appointed Jaleesa as associate pastor and privately counseled her to channel her considerable passion, ambition and creativity solely on the goal of increasing the fold and the fortunes of the church.

And the devil? He has kept his distance from Bethel and is not expected to visit again for a long, long time to come.

A Party for Allen

There is truth in the phrase "six degrees of separation." This last story brings together several of the characters you've met in this collection and shrinks those six degrees to three and in some cases to one.

Clay Johnson

Allen is dying. It's kidney failure—a roll of the genetic dice that's affected way too many folks in our family. Grandma, Dad, Uncle Henry and four cousins have transitioned off the planet during my lifetime because of this disease. Now it's my brother's turn.

He was twenty-two when he got his first kidney transplant. Now, after two more transplants and a maddening variety of pills, it's down to dialysis sessions three times a week. They're the only thing keeping him alive because this last kidney is failing. His doctors have given him three to six months. So, Allen and his husband, Harrison, decided to plan a celebration of life while he's still here and they can both enjoy it.

When they sat me down to break the news, I was devastated. I'd always known losing my brother was a possibility, but I'm not ready to see it become a reality.

Allen tried to lighten the mood, saying, “We’re celebrating now ’cause when I go, I plan to go quietly and be cremated. You’ll get a vial of ashes to keep for Sara. If she becomes an astronaut, she can fly ’em into space like they did for Jimmy Doohan—you know, the guy who played Scotty on Star Trek? Harrison’s going to have the rest made into a diamond to give him something hard to remember me by.”

Allen winked and grinned. Harrison rolled his eyes. I laughed.

Allen and my granddaughter Sara have a deep bond. Allen is one neutrino short of being a full-on Trekker. As soon as Sara could sit upright, he’d plop her on his lap and they’d watch Star Trek reruns all weekend, every weekend.

My brother, God love ’im, is at the center of an astonishing number of human intersections from his vintage clothing business to city council to community theater to a youth group at the local YMCA. We’re all proud of him.

We grew up in Virginia with my dad, followed by a couple of stepfathers after he died. Mom kept marrying nice guys, but they kept dying off. Lucky for us, they had good insurance policies. Mom, Allen and I never really wanted for much, except relief from the White folks. Our Black community was tight; we all looked out for one another. Given the times, we had to.

And Mom’s here. She took the train up from Virginia. We told her to stay home and take it easy, even offered to send pictures and video, but she is one stubborn lady. She reminds me of the old saying, “Just ’cause there’s snow on the roof, don’t mean the fire’s out in the boiler.” That’s Mom—one fiercely determined woman.

Lucille Jenkins

I was tore up after Allen an’ Clay called tellin’ me not to worry. Stay home an’ take it easy, they said. Humph! You’d think my sons would know me better ’n that! I told ’em I’d be there to plan the menu an’ make sure the food was up to my standards.

They knew better'n to try an' stop me. I may be old, but I'm still breathin' an' on the right side a the ground! People tellin' me I cain't or shouldn't do somethin' ain't never stopped me when my mind was made up.

If Allen wants to go out in style, then I'm gonna help. If food is love, then I'm makin' sure the food at this party talks loud an' clear about my love for him. Today, I'm gonna celebrate, not mourn. I'll mourn later, in private. Then I'll cry an' remember. Then I'll reach out an' touch his picture an' whisper, "Farewell, Allen. Goodbye."

But not now. Not today.

All of Allen's favorites are on the table, an' ain't nobody countin' calories tonight! It's amazin'. They's two big Dolphins carved outta ice sittin' in the center. Between 'em is a baby picture of Allen with African violets, ivy an' baby's breath all round. Allen's beamin' his best week ol' smile. It mighta been gas, but I'm sayin' it's a smile.

For the meat eaters, we got crispy fried chicken, country BBQ ribs an' smoked ham. They's meatless Hoppin' John for the vegetarians. The side dishes lookin' good too. I see collard greens, candied yams an' the mellow yellows of potato salad, corn bread an' macaroni an' cheese. The dessert table's got peach cobbler, pound cake, banana puddin' an' my nutmeg-glazed gingerbread from my ancestor Rebecca's book, *The Art of Nutmeg Cookery*. It's all lookin' like a grand New Year's Day Lucky Meal we used to make for folks down South. I am lucky to be celebratin' Allen's life with my family tonight.

He always was a good boy, but when he tol' me he liked boys, I didn't understan' what he was sayin' or what he meant. Back then, we didn't have words like "gay" an' "comin' out" where we was livin.' It took him a while to make me understan', an' that left me flat out dumbfounded with no words 'ceptin' to tell him I loved him no matta what, an' that he betta not tell anyone. I tol' him he needed to git outta town an' go somewheres else if he wanted to be safe, 'cause he warn't gon' be safe either in our small, southern, Black churchgoing community or in the larger, southern, White churchgoing community. He went north after high school, an' the fear sittin' on my heart for him finally lifted. He was a good boy. Now he's a good man.

This is the third time I've come north. The first was for my brother Jeremiah's installation as pastor of Bethel AME. It was a joyful occasion for him. He traveled a long hard road to get his happy endin'. The second time was for Allen an' Harrison's wedding. Jeremiah married 'em. I still can't quite wrap my head around a man marryin' a man, but Harrison's a sweet soul, and they done made a good life together. At my age, I sure don't feel I have to understan' everythin', but as long as Allen's happy, I'm happy for him.

Last Mother's Day, he surprised me with an amazin' gift. See, Rebecca's cookbook been handed down through the generations since she got it published way back in 1856—an amazin' thing for a Black woman to do way back then. By the time it come to me, it was falling apart, pages stained, torn an' tattered from lovin' use. Allen knew I'd get all fit to be tied if it left my house for any reason, so he took pictures of the pages with his phone an' had a writer friend a his do it up on a computer. They made me a bran' new copy that'll last another hunnerd years or so. Now ain't that somethin'!

Claudette Boyd

My life as an event decorator is a post-menopausal zest, a quit-the-job-and-live-the-dream kind of thing. It was slow going until Allen and Harrison hired me to plan their wedding. Most everyone I know says that if you believe the "six degrees of separation" theory and live in this city, you are no more than three degrees away from Allen—and only one degree if you're Black! That one degree helped my business, Creative Occasions, take off. Now I can pay Connie, Ardell and Frankie to staff my events. They're sister-friends from my book club. I like keeping things local and in the family, and these women are family.

We're holding Allen's party at the Pond House in Memorial Park. He picked it because, in addition to a cozy café and dining room walls decorated by local artists, it has a large outdoor patio with a view of the pond, an indoor carousel for kids to ride, and a variety of uniquely named meeting rooms. We booked the Haile Selassie Suite and joked that it'll be looking "sweet" indeed after we're finished with our planning. Allen wrote the program, selected the speakers, and told each one, "Be honest, be brief and you better be funny."

My mind knows everything's in order, but my gut always needs to take a last-minute walk-through to settle the butterflies in my stomach.

In the foyer, the guest registration book and the photos of Allen with friends, family, the mayor and the police chief are just as I pictured them. I look out the window to see Frankie in the parking lot, ready to direct traffic. I check in with Ardell and Connie at the main entrance. They'll greet folks as they arrive, then make sure they sign the guest book and get a program.

The invitation list is extensive and the RSVPs impressive. The only folks not coming are those sick, dead or out of the country. That includes Mariposa, Bob and the kids. They're in Turkey for an archaeological dig and a tour of the Middle East. Those who aren't here sent cards, texts and video messages. Next on my checklist is the room setup.

Allen's mom is at the buffet table. She gives me a big smile to let me know she's satisfied with the food before going off to join her family in the greenroom. Everyone else is already there: Allen and Harrison, Ms. Jenkins's brother Jeremiah, Allen's brother Clay, Clay's second wife Virgie, his son Scott, Scott's wife Maya, their daughter Sara, and last but not least, Harrison's parents, Richard and Cecilia.

My eyes take in the setup. The tables are decorated in indigo, white and gold, Allen's favorite color combination. I suggested a head table, but Allen nixed it—said he didn't want to be elevated above his guests. We decided on oval tables for eight, with Allen and his party at the front of the room but on the same level as everyone else. The chair covers and table toppers are white, the underskirts indigo, and the butterfly origami centerpieces white and gold. Chinese lanterns suspended from the ceiling give the whole room a mellow glow. I look over at the bandstand. The Global Drag Jazz Ensemble is warming up.

A text from Frankie says folks are starting to arrive. I take a deep breath, let it out slowly, and tell those butterflies in my stomach to fly in formation. I give the band a nod. *It's go time!*

Delores Gray

Bo Dayscious asks, "Dee, you ready to roll?"

I nod in the affirmative and give Bo a thumbs up.

"Okay, ladies... Let's hit it!" Bo signals the others, and we start our first set with the jazz standard "Come Rain or Come Shine."

Bo Dayscious is on drums, Charity Balls plays a mean bass, Ida B. Wylde tickles the ivories, and Coco D. Lite plays the flute. They've been performing in full drag for years, and frankly, I felt dowdy in their company until they took me shopping and fixed my makeup. I love them.

They heard me sing at Allen's wedding and asked me to join the ensemble. I told them I'd love to. I recently finished therapy and was looking for something positive to get involved in. See, my life got real heavy, and I went off one day in the cafeteria at work. After I got out of the loony bin, Charlaine, my sister-friend, suggested I see Doc Rutledge and now, most days, I'm managing pretty well.

Singing keeps me grounded. When I sing, I feel whole and complete—a new feeling for me. Another reason I'm managing is the drag queens. They're full of glitter, glitz and gossip. They can throw shade and spill the tea with the best of the best on *RuPaul's Drag Race*. But make no mistake... They are serious musicians.

I'm glad the first song is slow and mellow. It gives me time to calm my nerves and get a feel for the energy of the room as the guests mingle.

My tummy does a little flip-flop when I spot Doc Rutledge. Yes, I had a crush on him during therapy. What woman wouldn't crush on the handsome doctor helping her put herself back together?

A stab of envy pulses through me when his ex-wife comes in. I heard they're working on getting back together. I don't know the whole story, but gurrrrl, if he were mine, I'd a held onto him so tight, even light wouldn't find a way to get between us. Oh, well! I guess the grass is always greener in someone else's yard.

Allen Johnson

Harrison looks sad. I know he's thinking about life without me. I'd give anything to spare him what he's going to go through after I'm gone. But there's nothing to be done. I've known for a while this would be how I'd leave the planet. It's ironic... Ever since our ancestors arrived in this country, we've survived enslavement, Jim Crow, poverty, segregation, prejudice and the culture shock of living with the north's subtle racism. But there is no running away from this disease, and Harrison will have to find a way to live the rest of his life without me.

We met in our freshman year computer science course. I hated it. Harrison loved it because it would help him with his architecture studies. Our friendship began when he offered to help me with my assignments. In sophomore year, he'd drag me to museums and old buildings. I'd majored in political science, so I dragged him to voter rights meetings and rallies. By then, we had come out to each other and fallen in love.

When I knew for sure we'd have a future together, I introduced him to Clay and then took him to Virginia to meet Mom.

That went well because my family has known about me since high school. Harrison was another matter. He hadn't come out to his parents, so simultaneously telling them he was gay and bringing his Black boyfriend home to meet them would have been a stretch, probably more than either of us was ready for. So he did it in stages.

By the end of our junior year, he had come out to his parents. He was expecting shock and disapproval. What he got was anything but, and it threw him for a loop. Not only were they absolutely fine with it, they actually seemed relieved. Same response when they met me. Both of us were puzzled until we saw his DNA results from the kit I gave him for our first wedding anniversary. Life sure can turn on a dime!

I'm glad his parents are here today because Harrison is going to need their support after I'm gone.

Clay

I look at my brother and Harrison. They've been partners for years and decided to get married after the state recognized marriage as a union between two people who love each other, period.

It made no never mind to me that Allen was with a White man. I thought maybe Mom would have some reservations, her growing up and living in the racially segregated South, but she dealt with Allen being gay pretty well, so I figured she'd get used to Harrison being White. And indeed, she took it in stride. We all breathed a sigh of relief, figuring this would be the last of the family surprises.

Then Allen gave Harrison a DNA kit for their first wedding anniversary. See, Harrison was adopted, and his mom and dad never told him anything about his biological parents. Despite years of searching, he couldn't find out anything on his own either. He grew up with a White family in a White suburb as a White boy until the results came back and he got the surprise of his life. He may look White, but it turns out he's fifty-one percent sub-Saharan African, forty-six percent European, and three percent Native American. Talk about finding your roots!

He was astonished but not upset. He had questions. Coming out as gay to his parents had been tough enough, but now he needed to find out if they'd known he was mixed-race and hadn't told him—or, if they didn't know, how they would feel about him when they learned. That called for a family meeting. First, Allen and Harrison came over to talk to Virgie and me to get some advice. After dinner and a few drinks, Virgie suggested they go see Doc Rutledge and bring Harrison's parents with them.

They did. Turns out Harrison's parents did know but didn't tell him because they thought he'd have an easier life as a White man. When Harrison told them he was gay, they were okay with it because their only worry up to that point had been the possibility he might produce a Black grandchild when he married. Needless to say, those issues kept them in Rutledge's office for several sessions.

I look around the room. Allen is and always has been the center of attention, with his classy, intelligent, kind vibe. Being confined to a wheelchair doesn't hold him back. He looks dapper and fashionable despite being thin and sallow. It's clear he's fading away from us. I'm going to miss him something terrible, but right now, I need to be upbeat as we wait for Claudette to let us know when it's time to make our family entrance.

Claudette

Our guests are drinking cocktails and making small talk. All of them are people Allen loves and who love him right back: family, friends and a few dysfunctional others that Allen has worked with or befriended.

Allen has a talent for taking in strays and treating them like family. And if that sounds judgmental, it isn't. I'm one of those strays.

After I quit my job and started my fabric and textile business, I was living on canned tuna fish from the local food pantry until I met Allen at a Chamber of Commerce networking event. After hearing my story, he suggested I consider expanding my business to include event designing and then asked me to plan his wedding.

That was five years ago, and he's still recommending me to anyone who needs an elegant event decorated. I'm going to miss him when he leaves us, but right now I need to make sure this celebration goes off without a hitch.

Allen

I've made my peace with death. First, I researched the five stages of grief: denial, anger, bargaining, depression and acceptance. I went to Doc Rutledge to work through the first four. For the last, I hired a lawyer to write a will and manage my last requests. I have no regrets except that I'll need to do my dancing in this wheelchair, but I still have some moves left!

My phone pings. It's Claudette's text. I reach out and ask Sara to hold my hand. She puts her left hand in mine, clutches her Uhura doll with her right, looks up at me with those big brown eyes and says, "Unca Allen, when I'm big and fly my spaceship to the stars, can you come wif me?"

I lean in close, squeeze her hand and tell her, "Yes, baby girl, I can come with you. I've already made plans."

My family gathers around me. Harrison kisses the top of my head, and I smile.

It's on! Let's get my party started!

Discussion Questions

The stories in *Soul Food* focus on the themes of finding clarity, contentment and resilience in the complicated world the characters share. Compare and contrast these themes as you discuss these stories and consider the following questions.

General Discussion Questions

1. The connections throughout these stories begin with Rebecca and her cookbook and conclude with Allen's party. Did the author successfully weave the connections between the family and the friends they made? If so, how? And if not, why not?
2. Many of the stories deal with self-awareness and with challenges, choices and changes. Compare and contrast this theme in "A Recipe for Freedom" and "The Enlightenment of Franklin Rutledge." What challenges, choices and changes did the characters face? Was there one key moment that led them onto the path to making an important decision or was it a gradual development?
3. The stories are written from different points of view: male and female, first person (I) and third

person (she/he). Did the author successfully make these points of view authentic, clear and effective?

4. Why do you think the author chose the title *Soul Food* for this collection of stories? What would you have named this book?
5. Several of the stories contain elements of magical realism or strange phenomena presented in a real-world setting. Examples include “The Lateral Drift of Mariposa Jones,” “A Stitch in Time,” “1-800-555-MARY” and “The Devil Gets His Due.” How effective was this technique in moving the stories forward?
6. Were the characters believable in terms of how they reacted or responded to their situations? Give a few examples.
7. Which story had the greatest impact on you? Which story had the least? Why?

Recipe for Freedom

1. What were the social and cultural situations in the 1800s that complicated life for Rebecca and Margaret?
2. In what ways did Rebecca exhibit resilience when faced with the challenges of her personal life and her relationship with Margaret?
3. Which scenes in the story illustrate Rebecca’s level of self-awareness and clarity about her situation?

A Grave Situation

1. What personality traits enabled Lucille Jenkins to “get somewheres in this life”?
2. Why do you think Sam was unable to look past things he couldn’t control? Do you believe if he did, that might have led to a longer life?

3. How did Homer's perception of his status in the community prevent him from dealing openly with Lucille?

Waiting for Grace

1. Jeremiah's faith and his calling faced a serious challenge. Why do you think he took so long to work through it?
2. In what ways did his sister and the train conductor help him reach a solution?
3. This story contained elements of magical realism. How effective was this technique in moving the story forward?

How Sadie Smoked 'Em

1. How did the trifecta of racism, sexism and workers' rights impact Sadie's life as a young woman?
2. Can you name one or two occupations in which those same issues can be seen today?
3. What gave Sadie the courage to step into the leadership role that changed her life?

The Lady in Red

1. How might you explain Marilyn's lifelong attraction to the Barrington estate?
2. Discuss the difference between Basil and Meredith's response to the results of the DNA test Basil took.
3. What do their reactions say about their levels of self-awareness and acceptance?

Mama Rose's Kitchen

1. Are you sympathetic to the character of Wyatt Barrington? If so, why?

2. In discussing the new voting rights bill, Maybelle told Brian that "The letter of the law is clear as a bell. My problem was and is with the spirit behind it." What did she mean by this?
3. Do you think Wyatt and Maybelle will eventually overcome the challenges still facing them at the end of the story?

The Lateral Drift of Mariposa Jones

1. What was the purpose of Mariposa's mystical experience?
2. Why do you think Mariposa spent so much of her life giving in to the needs of her mother, her husband, her job and her children?
3. How did sharing her dilemma with her dog, her brother and Miss Millie help her gain clarity and build the resilience she needed to make a change?

A Stitch in Time

1. Can you identify one or more core beliefs that kept Claudette imprisoned in her well of negativity?
2. How did her passion for fabric and design help her find a measure of contentment in spite of her struggles?
3. At what point in listening to Rebecca Primus's story does Claudette gain self-awareness?

1-800-555-MARY

1. What were the key challenges that Delores faced?
2. Why do you think the Mary billboard upset Delores?
3. How did calling the number on the Mary billboard connect Delores with herself?

The Enlightenment of Franklin Rutledge

1. Why do you think Franklin had such a deep need for control?
2. How did that need affect his marriage?
3. How did watching the Hobsons's communication with each other deepen Franklin's understanding of what he needed to do to make peace with his ex-wife?

Guess Who's Coming to Dinner

1. How does Virgie view her relationship with her family?
2. How and when during dinner does Virgie gain clarity about her perspective of her family?
3. What role does Merle play in Virgie's change of heart?

The Well-Wrapped Life

1. What drove Martha Rae Edmonds to make an appointment with Franklin Rutledge?
2. Can you list a few reasons why she sought perfection in her life?
3. Why do you think Franklin was drawn to Martha Rae?

Warrior Women of the Third Sunday

1. Who was your favorite character in this story and why?
2. What do you think about Nicole's mother's Rules of Marriage for women?
3. If you are in a book club, how does it compare to the one in this story?

The Devil Gets His Due

1. Humor is an integral part of this story. Were you able to find humor in any of the other stories in this book? Which ones?
2. How can humor help a person gain clarity, contentment and resilience?
3. How did Webster Lee's heart attack change his life?

A Party for Allen

1. When a challenge can't be overcome with intention or action, the only path is to find acceptance. How does Allen find it?
2. The connections in *Soul Food* begin with Rebecca and her cookbook and conclude with Allen's party. Which connections between the characters in the book or in this story stood out to you? Why?
3. How would you like your friends and family to celebrate your life?

Glossary of Cultural Terms

In reading the stories in this book, you may have encountered words and terms that are unfamiliar to you. Here are the historical roots and meanings of some of them.

Big House

The plantation owner's home during the legal institution of human enslavement, which was first legalized in Massachusetts in 1641 lasted until the end of the Civil War in 1865.

Brown Paper Bag Test

A form of colorism used by some Black groups to exclude dark-skinned people from fraternities, organizations and other social clubs by comparing their skin tone to the color of a brown paper bag. The discriminatory practice continued well into the twentieth century.

Hoppin' John

A dish of black-eyed peas and rice (with or without meat). The first written "receipt" for Hoppin' John appeared in *The Carolina Housewife* in 1847, a cookbook from Charlestonian Sarah Rutledge. Learn more in *The History of Hoppin' John* by Allyson Jones. (bluffton.com/history-hoppin-john)

Miss Ann

A term originally used in the South by the Black community to describe a White woman who employs Black women in the role of domestic workers.

New Year's Day Lucky Meal

According to Southern folklore, eating certain foods on New Year's Day, like Hoppin' John, collard greens and cornbread, guaranteed good luck, wealth and prosperity throughout the year.

Race men

An older term referring to a person who dedicates their activism to working for the betterment of Black people.

Southern Rights men

During the early 1860s, this group of White men were dedicated to protecting states' rights and limiting the northern states' attempts to curb the spread of slavery.

Underground Railroad

A network of people, both White and free Blacks, who worked together to establish routes and safe houses during the early- to mid-nineteenth century. It was used by enslaved Black people to escape to free states and Canada.

Up South

As opposed to the Deep South, Up South refers to states like North Carolina and Virginia, which are closer to the northern states but have strong ties to Southern culture.

Acknowledgments

There are so many people and resources to acknowledge and thank for their contributions to the creation of this book.

First, I need to offer a note of deep appreciation for the three women whose wisdom and good counsel have influenced my life and provided grist for milling this collection of short stories. They are my mother, Margaret Gibbs; my great-aunt, Lucille Garnett; and my cousin Ella Garnett. Their messages about the importance of independence and self-reliance for women are reflected in and shine through several stories in this book. I will be forever grateful for those life lessons, as they have carried me through more than a few tough times.

A big "thank you" to my friend and book club buddy, Cheryl Curtis, who graciously allowed me to use her poem "Warrior Women of the Third Sunday" in my story of the same name. She wrote the poem for our book club, The Palm Society (Poetry, Art, Literature and Music). Thank you, Cheryl.

A huge debt of gratitude goes to my writing family, Journey Writers, Inc. (journeywriters.org) Over the past two years, during our Saturday workshops, they listened to me read every story in this book. Their feedback, constructive comments and suggestions were invaluable. They are the best!

The *CT Literary Anthology* gets my gratitude and thanks for publishing two of these stories. "1-800-555-MARY" was published in 2020 and “Guess Who’s Coming to Dinner?” in their 2021 edition.

I would be remiss if I didn’t acknowledge the impact that Gloria Naylor’s writing has had on me. She was an American novelist, and two of her books, *The Women of Brewster Place* and *Bailey’s Café*, introduced me to the short story cycle, a form of writing that offers the reader a larger story crafted through a series of connected stories, each with a definitive beginning, middle and end.

Another big thank you goes to the wide variety of research sources I consulted to help me find ways to link and connect the timelines and characters. As a result, much of what I read served as inspiration for several of the stories, particularly, “How Sadie Smoked ’Em,” “The Lady in Red” and “A Stitch in Time.”

This book, like my last one, is ever grateful for the publishing expertise of Emerald Lake Books and the work of Tara Alemany and Mark Gerber. Tara’s editing, marketing and promotional guidance, and expertise are amazing. Mark’s art direction and understanding of color, design and formatting resulted in a finished product that feels alive and soulful. Thank you both.

My deepest gratitude goes to those who endorsed this book. I can’t thank them enough for making time in their lives to read a draft and write so many kind and heartfelt words to support this book.

Most of all, thank you to my readers. I hope this book provides you with thought-provoking inspiration, information and entertainment.

About the Author

Beth Gibbs is an award-winning author, speaker and self-awareness trainer who has held management and executive positions in media, higher education and nonprofit organizations. She holds a master's degree in Communications from the University of Hartford and another in Yoga Therapy and Mind/Body Health from Lesley University in Cambridge, Massachusetts.

Currently, Beth is "free-tired" and writing fiction and personal growth nonfiction for mainstream audiences. Her goal is to inspire, inform and entertain. Her published writing includes short stories, blog posts, newsletters and magazine articles on the benefits of personal growth, self-awareness, yoga, mindfulness and meditation. She has published a book entitled *Enlighten Up! Finding Clarity, Contentment and Resilience in a Complicated World* and a children's book called *Ogi Bogi, The Elephant Yogi: Stories About Yoga for Children*. Her blog can be found at bethgibbs.com.

Beth established The Garnett Gibbs Family Fund at the Hartford Foundation for Public Giving in memory of her parents. The purpose of the fund is to support healthy living programs in the greater Hartford, Connecticut, region for at-risk populations and people of all ages, especially programs for children in public schools and community settings. She founded and continues to support The Wake Up and Relax! yoga program for Hartford's Camp Courant, Inc. that serves urban children ages five to thirteen.

She is a member of Journey Writers, Inc., a not-for-profit organization that provides a safe space for writers to share their work and to give and receive honest, constructive, encouraging feedback. The group also offers a variety of programs for members to present their work to a wider audience.

Her favorite quote has been tacked to several refrigerators and survived at least three moves over the past twenty years. It is:

> *Voyager, there are no bridges. One builds them as one walks.*
>
> —Gloria Anzaldúa

If you're interested in having Beth speak to your group or organization, you can contact her at emeraldlakebooks.com/gibbs.

www.ingramcontent.com/pod-product-compliance
Lightning Source LLC
Chambersburg PA
CBHW061447210726
48287CB00007B/2396

* 9 7 8 1 9 4 5 8 4 7 6 6 0 *